Sinister Cinnamon Buns

By

J Lee Mitchell

Sinister Cinnamon Buns

By J Lee Mitchell

First Edition

Copyright © 2018 by J Lee Mitchell

Dedication

To Bob. This book would never have been possible without all your love, support, and encouragement. Thank you for always being there for me. I love you more than you will ever know.

TABLE OF CONTENTS

Chapter 1

The screen door flew open with a thud, startling Rene and Evie as they huddled around a small TV watching *Country Cooking With Macie*. Liddy Lou Cormier stomped up to them, snatched the remote off the counter, and switched off the TV. She slammed the remote down on the counter so hard it cracked. Without saying a word, she stomped out the swinging doors leading to the Red Herring Inn's dining room, letting them smack shut behind her.

Q'Bita Block stood just inside the doorway of her cooking school, Culinary Forensics, which doubled as the kitchen for her family's inn. Rene and Evie stared at her waiting for an explanation as to what had Liddy Lou so upset.

Q'Bita's hands were firmly planted on her slender hips, and her dark curls swayed as she spoke.

"Seriously, you two? Did you really think it was a good idea to have Nana come home and catch you watching the show that started this whole mess in the first place?"

Before she could continue, her brother-in-law, Rene, interrupted.

"Great ghost of Greta Garbo, how bad was your meeting with the publishers? I've never seen Liddy Lou so ornery. Look at this," he said, picking up the ruined remote. "She cracked it like an egg."

Q'Bita sighed as she sat down next to Evie. She reached for a cherry crumb bar and fought back tears as she tried to speak, her voice cracking as she mumbled, "... just not right. How am I going to fix this?"

Q'Bita sighed again then squared her shoulders. Now was not the time to be weak.

Evie put her arm around Q'Bita and gave her a tender squeeze.

"Don't fret, Q'Bita. Liddy Lou's just blowing off some steam. No matter how bad this seems, your nana has weathered far worse storms. This one will pass, same as the others, and she'll still be standing like the stubborn oak she's always been."

Rene, who'd been uncharacteristically quiet since Liddy Lou's meltdown, couldn't contain himself a second longer.

"Um, hello. Could you two put the kibosh on the Hallmark moment and please tell me what happened at your meeting? I need details, people."

Q'Bita tried not to laugh as Evie swatted at Rene and shushed him while he feigned offense. Her brother's husband might be a bit dramatic at times, but his flamboyance could always lift her out of a funk.

"Okay. As I'm sure you've already guessed, the meeting didn't go well. The publishers received a cease-and-desist order from the law firm of Winston, Wheaton, and Wilbur on behalf of the Dixons. The order requires the publishers to stop all current and future production of *Cooking The Cormier Way*. The publishers are hesitant to engage in a protracted legal battle, so they've decided to shelf Nana's book until further notice. They were, however, gracious enough to inform us that we are welcome to seek our own legal counsel if we want to challenge the Dixons."

Evie Newsome slapped the marble counter and stood up. "You have got to be kidding me. Who the hell do those Dixons think they are? Everyone in Castle Creek knows Macie Dixon is a fraud. The girl couldn't fry an egg on a hundred-degree sidewalk at high noon even if she had a damn frying pan and a spatula for hands."

Rene snorted and rolled his eyes.

"And people say I'm overly dramatic."

Evie threw Rene a look like a rattlesnake about to strike then sat down taking Q'Bita's hand in hers.

"I'm sorry, Q'Bita. As much as it pains me to admit Rene's right, maybe I'm a little too fired up. I know how hard it was for Liddy Lou to share those recipes and stories from the Cormier family wedding books and it breaks my heart that her book got shelved. I've spent my whole life here in Castle Creek watching the Dixons use their money to manipulate their way to the top. Isn't there anything we can do?"

Q'Bita shook her head.

"I'm afraid not. I'll talk to my parents and see if they've ever run into anything like this with one of their books, but for now it seems our only option is to take this whole mess to court. In the meantime, Macie Dixon is free to keep using the recipes she stole from us."

"Speaking of recipes, do you think Liddy Lou will calm down in time to teach tonight's class? I'm not sure we should let her near knives when she's this worked up," Evie said.

"I think she'll be fine. We just need to give her a few more hours."

"Well, I'm taking tonight's class, so I'll be there if things get out of hand and you need some muscle," Rene said.

"Oh, a lot of help you'd be. What are you going to do, Princess Rose Bowl, wave Liddy Lou into submission?"

"My, my, Evie, aren't we catty today? Words can wound you know?"

Q'Bita and Evie both laughed as Rene picked the topping off another cherry crumb bar.

"Oh, you big drama queen, you know I love you. I'm just pecking at you to lighten things up a little around here.

Evie and Rene kept up their back-and-forth until Liddy Lou reappeared.

"Q'Bita, darling, I hate to spring this on you at the last minute but I'm really not feeling up to dealing with people right now. Would you and Evie mind terribly if I didn't teach tonight?"

"It won't be the same without you, Nana, but Evie and I don't mind holding down the fort for a night."

"Thank you, girls. I think some alone time will do me good."

Liddy Lou gave them a half smile and left without saying

goodbye.

Chapter 2

Most nights Q'Bita loved teaching, but tonight her heart wasn't in it. She watched the last of the participants shuffle in and take their seats as Evie made her way to the front of the room to join her.

Q'Bita took a deep breath, flipped on her mic, and began the first class she'd held without her nana since they'd opened Culinary Forensics. She just hoped she didn't start crying before she finished the announcements.

"Hello, everyone. For those who don't know me, I'm Q'Bita Block, and this is my lovely and talented co-instructor, Evie Newsome. We want to welcome you all to the Red Herring Inn and Culinary Forensics, where our goal is to take some of the mystery out of cooking by teaching you the science behind food in order to prevent culinary crimes."

As usual, a little bit of laughter and a few groans at her corniness rippled through the crowd, and Q'Bita started to feel a better.

"Unfortunately, my nana cannot be with us tonight, but we are very excited that my brother-in-law, Rene, has graciously agreed to step in and help out."

Rene grabbed the corners of his fake-fur, ruffled, leopard skin-print apron, curtsied, then gave the class his best prom court wave.

Q'Bita finished the rest of the announcements and got class started. Things were going well until they took the cookies out of the oven and discovered that not everyone had been successful.

Max Bower and Rene were in a huddle having a serious-looking discussion as Q'Bita approached them.

"Hi, fellas. How'd the cookies turn out?"

"I guess that depends on whether or not you like the taste of soap," Max replied.

Q'Bita picked up a cookie, took a nibble, and knew in an instant what had happened.

"Max, you didn't measure everything according to the recipe. There's too much baking soda in these."

Max gave her a surprised look.

"How did you know?"

"Max, how many times do I have to tell you? I have super powers, you can't fool me. I have a Master's Degree in Food Science and graduated top of my class from culinary school. You're going to have to try a lot harder to pull one over on me. Too much baking soda and not enough acid produces a metallic, or soapy, taste that can be rather off-putting in a cookie."

Max laughed and said to Rene, "She's good. I try to get her every class, and every class, she figures me out."

"Wait. You did this on purpose? What in the name of Betty Crocker where you thinking, Max? Q'Bita, when do we serve the wine? My palate needs to be cleansed before it's permanently damaged by these dreadful soap wafers."

"Sorry, Rene, we don't serve wine with this class."

"What, no wine? You could have told me before I agreed to help. This constitutes a hostile work environment and I resign, effective immediately."

Max laughed as Rene marched off to sulk in the corner.

"Boy, he's an excitable fella, that one. I hope he's not too upset. I come to these classes just to try and stump you. I've never met anyone who knows as much about cooking and how it works as you, Q'Bita. If you ever decide to settle down, I could use a wife who can cook."

Q'Bita blushed and wagged her finger at Max, who may not have been able to make a cookie, but he never failed to make a pass at Q'Bita, or her nana.

She made her way around the rest of the class sampling cookies and giving advice on how to fix any of the mishaps. Most people had done a great job and enjoyed the class, which made her wish all the more that her nana had been there to enjoy it with them.

Chapter 3

Hadleigh Banks glanced over the top of her iPad, watching the day's carnage unfold in its usual fashion. Macie was standing behind the stove screeching at the food stylist, barking orders at the camera crew, and teetering on the edge of her next explosion while production people scurried everywhere like scared little rats nervously waiting to see whom Macie would fire next.

Being the personal assistant to a spoiled, clueless egomaniac was far from Hadleigh's idea of a dream job. Working for Macie Dixon and trying to keep her own agenda a secret was exhausting and hadn't gotten her any closer to what she really wanted. A loud crash and the sound of broken glass jarred Hadleigh out of her introspection.

"Which one of you imbeciles thought it would be appropriate to stage this segment with cheap-ass, mismatched dessert plates? I am trying to launch a freaking lifestyle brand here, not champion some junk-shop, bohemian aesthetic. Clean this mess up and restage this segment with pieces from the Macie Dixon Line. I will be in my dressing room and I do not want to be disturbed until you people pull your heads out of your asses."

Everyone was frozen, staring at Macie, until she marched off the set bellowing for Hadleigh.

"I am over here, Macie. What do you need?"

Macie lurched to a stop and rounded on Hadleigh.

"Why does this level of incompetence continue to happen daily? I pay you to attend to details. I do not have time for incessant ridiculousness. I need to keep myself in tune with my creative harmonics and be free and open to my muse."

Hadleigh was barely able to refrain from blurting out a sarcastic reply. Instead, she stood still and counted to ten in her mind. She cast a glace in the direction of the crew as they scrambled to clean up the stack of plates Macie had tossed to the floor. She momentarily locked eyes with Macie's food stylist, Patti Becker, and mouthed a silent, "Sorry."

It was times like this Hadleigh questioned how she and Macie shared a parent. Not that anyone but Hadleigh knew that at this point, and she wasn't ready to share this secret just yet. For now, she would just have to bite the bullet and let her half-sister treat her like the hired help, which, technically, she was.

"Hadleigh!"

Macie's voice could chew through your neck skin and burrow itself all the way to your bone marrow. Hadleigh steeled herself, slapped on her faux-obedient look, and set off behind Macie muttering to herself, "Stay calm, Hadleigh. You need this job."

Chapter 4

Q'Bita popped a tray of rosemary cheddar biscuits into the oven and set the timer. The kitchen was soon filled with the scent of warm, buttery dough, which made it hard for her to stay focused on writing recipe descriptions for next month's cooking classes. She was just about to make herself a cup of blueberry rooibos tea from her special stash when Jamie Gross arrived for his shift.

Jamie wasn't blood, but he had been fostered by Liddy Lou, and the Blocks considered him family. In the two years since Q'Bita had moved from Spain to Castle Creek she and Jamie had become inseparable. Jamie had a way about him that made her smile even when her heart was hurting. After their meeting with the publisher yesterday, things around the Red Herring Inn had been anything but upbeat, and Q'Bita was happy to see him. She gave Jamie a huge hug, and he hit her with his usual greeting.

"What's shaking, Q'B-doll?"

Q'Bita was trying to decide if she should spill the details of their meeting or let Rene give Jamie the full dramatic retelling when Liddy Lou came in from the garden.

Jamie laid a big, sloppy kiss on Liddy Lou, and she suggested he save all that mess for the ladies before extracting herself from his embrace.

Jamie took a step back, crossed his arms over his body, and asked, "Okay, what did I miss? I'm sensing some hostility."

Liddy Lou made a face like she'd smelled something gone bad and waved her hands around in front of herself trying to ignore Jamie's question.

"Nothing for you to worry yourself about. Besides, I'm sure Rene is busting at the seams to tell you all about it."

"Not so fast, little Mama. If something is troubling you, then it's better I hear it from you. You know if I hear it from Rene it will be blown so far out of proportion I'll be ready to knee-cap someone before he even finishes his story."

Liddy Lou let out a half-hearted chuckle. "Now y'all know that I seldom condone violence, but today I just might hand you the bat and look the other way."

Jamie shifted his gaze from Liddy Lou to Q'Bita, his face tight with concern.

"Okay. Seriously, ladies, what happened?"

Liddy Lou shook her head and started towards the swinging doors leading to the dining room. "Maybe it's best if Q'Bita fills you in. I've finally gotten my blood pressure just under the stroke zone, and if it goes back up again I just might do something I can't undo."

The buzz of the oven timer was just the distraction Liddy Lou needed to make a speedy exit from the kitchen.

Jamie turned to Q'Bita. "What the hell was that all about?"

Q'Bita sat the golden, buttery biscuits on the counter and closed the oven door.

"We had a meeting with the publishers yesterday, and the Dixons have decided to take legal action against us. Long story short, *Cooking The Cormier Way* has been placed on indefinite hold."

"Can they actually do that? I thought Liddy Lou had a contract."

"She does, but the contract states that the recipes in the book will be original, unpublished recipes, and the legal team at the publishing house is afraid that publishing any of the recipes Macie has already used on her show might become fodder for a future legal battle with the Dixons."

Jamie grabbed one of the steaming hot biscuits from the tray and stuffed it in his mouth.

"I still don't understand," he mumbled through a wad of half-chewed biscuit. "Isn't the book a compilation of recipes handed down through your family from their wedding books? If the recipes are already in the wedding books, isn't that enough to prove they originated with your family and not Macie Dixon?"

"Hold that thought," Q'Bita said as she grabbed two glasses from the cupboard and filled them with ice, blackberry tea, and a shot of rosemary simple syrup. She sat the glasses down on the counter and moved the tray of biscuits closer to the iced tea.

"Come on, sit down with me and have a snack. I already checked the reservations this morning and we don't have anyone checking in until later this evening, so we have plenty of time, and it will make me feel better to talk this all out with you."

Jamie and Q'Bita were just settling in when Q'Bita's parents entered the kitchen. Kari Block greeted each of them with a hug and double kiss, one for each cheek. Tom Block waved a quick hello and, as usual, went directly for the still warm biscuits.

"Good," said Q'Bita. "You two are just in time. I'll grab two more iced teas. I was about to fill Jamie in on my and Nana's visit with the publishers yesterday. I was hoping the two of you might be able to shed some light on any options Nana might have."

Kari buried her face in her hands and shook her head side to side.

"Ugh, this is so horrible. I feel partly responsible for this whole mess. Your nana really struggled with the decision about whether or not to share our family recipes, and I can't help but think we might have avoided all this drama if I hadn't pushed her so hard."

Tom Block was half-way through his second biscuit but paused to interject, "I know that things seem bad right now but if we've learned anything while churning out twenty-three books and coaching countless clients through the publishing process, it's that nothing ever comes easily in this business."

Kari nodded in agreement. "Your father's right, publishing can be brutal at times, and we've been really fortunate so far to have never run into this kind of a legal issue, so, sadly, we can't be much help."

"So that's it, then? Are y'all saying there isn't anything we can do

12

to fix this?"

Jamie looked from Tom to Kari and then to Q'Bita, his eyes clouding up and lower lip trembling slightly.

"Liddy Lou took me in when everyone else in my life had completely given up on me. I love that cantankerous old goat, and I can't stand to see her hurt and upset. There has to be something we can do."

Q'Bita got up, grabbed the pitcher of blackberry iced tea from the fridge, and placed it on a tray with the rosemary simple syrup. She sat the tray on the counter next to the last few biscuits and refilled everyone's glass.

Then she moved to the other side of the counter and hugged her bestie for the second time that day. She was suddenly overcome with a sense of appreciation for her nana's wisdom and foresight to buy the Red Herring Inn and bring them all home where they could work through the tough times as a family.

Chapter 5

Patti Becker could feel her heart beating in her ears, accompanied by a roaring noise that drowned out all the sound around her as she made her way down the hall towards her doom. The crew had played rock, paper, scissors to see who was going to be the unfortunate soul to go fetch Macie Dixon from her dressing room, and Patti had lost.

"I should have gone for throat punch instead of rock," she muttered to herself.

Patti paused for a moment just outside the door and swallowed hard. No sound was coming from the dressing room, and she said a silent prayer to the food gods that Macie had already gone back to the set. She was just about to knock when the door flew open and Patti found herself face to face with Macie.

"Why are you lurking, Patsy? Didn't I tell you idiots that I didn't want to be disturbed?"

Patti squared her shoulders and straightened her back, which put her at least three full inches taller than Macie Dixon. "It's Patti, and you said not to disturb you until we re-staged the set, which we have. We need to wrap for the day by five so the sooner we get you on set the sooner we can get this episode put to bed."

Macie's face curled into a snarl. "This show is called *Country Cooking With Macie* for a reason, me! *I'm* the talent, it's *my* show, which means *I* say when we wrap, not you, not the crew. Me. Are we clear on that, Patsy?"

Patti choked back a snarky reply and tucked her hands into her back pockets where she could give Macie the bird without getting fired. Macie slammed the door in her face without another word. As Patti turned away, cussing under her breath, she noticed Macie's assistant standing behind her.

"Sorry, she's in one of her moods today."

Hadleigh gave Patti a small, meek smile and said, "Go on back to the set. I'll get her majesty there as soon as I can."

Patti took a few steps then turned back to face Hadleigh. "Please understand this isn't directed towards you in any way, because God knows you have it even worse than we do, but someday Macie Dixon is going to mistreat one of us one time too many, and she's going to get what's coming to her. You can't treat people like they don't matter and not have to deal with the consequences of your actions at some point."

The look on Patti's face was pure hatred, and Hadleigh shuddered as Patti walked away.

Chapter 6

Hadleigh waited until Patti Becker turned the corner at the end of the hall before knocking on Macie's dressing room door. A few seconds later Macie yanked open the door.

"Look, Patsy," Macie snapped. She crinkled her surgically perfected nose and gave Hadleigh a disinterested look.

"Oh, it's you. Did you inspect the set and make sure those morons staged this segment with pieces from the Macie Dixon Line this time? If I go out there and every detail isn't perfect I just might shit-can the whole bunch of you. I can't even begin to tell you how sick I am of being the only person with a vision around here. It's no wonder successful entrepreneurs are often seen as unreasonable and demanding. It's completely frustrating, and exhausting, trying to find competent help some days."

Hadleigh stood in the doorway suppressing a smile, and a giggle, as she pictured herself bitch-slapping her smug, self-entitled sibling.

"Hadleigh, are you listening to me? God, sometimes I swear you pretend to be clueless just to boil my blister."

Hadleigh had reached her breaking point. Unable to stifle her laughter another second, she snorted like a piglet. Macie's expression quickly changed from disinterest to indignation.

"Really? Is this funny to you, Hadleigh? Because it's not funny to me. The Macie Dixon Line is my raison d'être, the love child I've carried inside myself and given painful birth to. I realize you're a just an assistant, but I expect—no, I demand—you have some respect for me and my vision."

From behind Hadleigh a deep, male voice interrupted Macie's lecture.

"If you want respect, you have to earn it, Macie, and you sure as hell aren't going to gain anyone's respect by stealing recipes and passing them off as your own."

Hadleigh turned to find a handsome, dark-skinned man she'd never met before standing just inches behind her. She hadn't heard anyone approach, but his timing was as impeccable as his sense of style. She thought to herself that it was no wonder she'd never met this delicious hunk of man-meat before. Hell, if he belonged to her she'd keep him well hidden from every other female in town, too.

Hadleigh couldn't help noticing that Macie's expression had turned from fury to fearful. Macie pushed past her, practically knocking her into the door frame. She grabbed the handsome stranger by the elbow and yanked him towards her dressing room, shoving him inside.

Macie started to shut the door but paused and said, "You're dismissed, Hadleigh. Tell the crew I will be there when I'm ready, and right now, I'm not ready." Macie then slammed the door in her face.

Hadleigh stood staring at the door for a minute. She couldn't make out what they were saying but she could tell they were having a very heated discussion. Hadleigh made a mental note to herself to find out just who this mystery man was and what he'd meant about stealing recipes and trying to pass them off as her own.

Chapter 7

Since moving to Castle Creek to join her family at the Red Herring Inn, Q'Bita had come to love sharing breakfast with her brother Beecher and his husband, Rene. They'd quickly fallen into a routine that included Q'Bita making coffee and biscuits or pastry while Beecher fed the Inn's growing flock of critters and grabbed the morning paper, and Rene spent the entire time primping himself.

As soon as they were all gathered, Rene would be proclaiming himself a hot mess and tear through the paper until he found the Heard About Town column, or gossip section, as Beecher liked to call it.

Q'Bita and Beecher would sip the coffee while Rene regaled them with every juicy bit of dirt on the who's who of Castle Creek.

Some people might find Rene's chitchat annoying first thing in the morning, but Q'Bita loved every second spent with her family. After all, who wouldn't love a two hundred eighty-five-pound, semi-hairy diva in a too-short, fuchsia-colored silk kimono as their breakfast companion? Okay, most people, but Q'Bita wasn't most people, and today's gossip just happened to be about Nana.

Rene let out a gasp that caught their attention.

"Holy Hettie Lamar, you two'd better prepare yourselves for this bombshell."

Rene's voice was several octaves above its usual caterwaul. Q'Bita leaned in closer as Beecher folded down the top of the sport section and said, "Do tell."

Rene threw him an exasperated look.

"If you two could settle yourselves and let me finish, I will."

Beecher, who hadn't gotten more than five words in edgewise since they'd met eight years ago, chuckled and waived his hand in a 'please go on' gesture.

Rene rolled his eyes, huffed in pseudo-indignation, and began reading from Spenser Penn's Heard About Town column. "I have it on very good authority that Castle Creek's own culinary darling, Macie Dixon, host of *Country Cooking With Macie* has had her reputation besmirched by none other than Red Herring Inn owner and Block Family matriarch, Liddy Lou Cormier. Rumor has it these two feisty females are having a bit of a row over whose recipes are whose, and things are now getting messy on a legal level. While I have no personal knowledge of who is in the right, one cannot help but take notice that *Country Cooking With Macie* is still airing new episodes each week but *Cooking The Cormier Way*, which was scheduled to be released next month, appears to have been placed on hold by the publisher."

Rene tossed the whole paper over his shoulder with a flurry of drama.

"Can you believe they actually printed that blasphemy? We should march down to their office, and Beecher should plow that blow hard in his Dixon shit-smeared nose. I mean, really, who reads this drivel? And even if they do, why would they believe a word this schmuck prints?"

Rene paused for a split second to inhale, and Beecher saw his chance.

"Um, Rene, you read that drivel. Besides, I think the best thing we can all do is keep our eyes and ears open and our mouths shut."

Rene interrupted, "Good Lord, Beecher, I thought Rolfie was the only neutered male in this family."

At the sound of his name, the twenty-pound Havana brown cat lifted his head from where he currently lay basking in a shaft of morning sun and cast them all a look that said he did not wish to be pulled into this discussion unless it ended in him being worshiped via offerings of thick-cut bacon.

Q'Bita chuckled, nodding in Rolfie's direction. "Sorry, your majesty, we did not mean to disturb your sleep."

As if he understood, Rolfie stretched his entire length, yawning wide to show a mouth full of meat-shredding teeth, and promptly returned to his solar-induced coma.

Rene sneered in the feline's direction.

"Oh, please, such drama."

Q'Bita laughed again. "I wonder where he learned that."

"Hush. I'm incensed here, and we need to get back to me. We cannot just sit back and let hacks like Spenser Penn malign this family and have the whole town believing that Macie Dixon is the victim. I just don't understand why you two aren't more worked up about this."

Beecher sighed, set the sports section aside, and rolled his eyes at Q'Bita.

"We are upset, Rene. We Blocks just have a different approach than most. The last thing we need to do is get things all stirred up while everyone is watching and waiting to see what we'll do next. I think the best thing any of us can do is focus on how to make this right."

Rene slapped the table with the palm of his hand.

"Well then, Sherlock, what's the plan? And please, be specific, so I know what to wear when we spring into action. The right shoe makes all the difference."

Beecher picked up the last bite of cranberry orange scone from his plate and tossed it towards Rolfie, who'd been startled by Rene's outburst and was now sitting a few feet away cleaning his inappropriate bits.

Rene shoved an enormous bite of scone slathered in citrus compound butter into his mouth and then tried to talk around it.

"I tell you what, why don't you two finish nourishing yourselves while I shower, and then we can brainstorm our next move?"

"Fine but don't take too long. Now that Rolfie's had a taste of scone he just might maul us to death for the rest of them," Q'Bita said.

Chapter 8

Liddy Lou was trying to decide if she wanted to wear the pearls her husband had given her for their last wedding anniversary before he passed, or the scarf Myra Thomas had given her for last year's secret Santa. She felt her spirits sag as she thought about how poor Myra had never made it to the New Year. A fall on the ice led to pneumonia that she just wasn't strong enough to fight.

She finally decided that she was depressed enough without bedecking herself in reminders of those she'd lost and settled on her purple hat with the peacock feathers in the band when her house phone rang. She knew before she even picked up that it was Evie Newsome. Evie was the only one who ever called her house phone. They had been best friends for decades, but unlike Evie, who preferred the farm life and simple things, which did not include computers or cell phones, Liddy Lou loved technology and gadgets and all the things that Evie found so complicated.

"Hiya, Evie. What's up?"

"Dag blamet, Liddy Lou. How'd you know it was me? What if I'd been some creepy deep-breather or a serial killer checking to see if you were home alone?"

"Oh, for God's sake, Evie, it's not like I live off the grid in isolation. The Red Herring Inn is staffed twenty-four seven, I'm surrounded by family, and we're booked solid with guests until the middle of next year. I couldn't be alone even if I wanted to."

There was a long pause before Evie spoke again. "Speaking of wanting to be left alone, I hate to be the bearer of bad news. I know you don't bother reading the Castle Creek Gazette since Rene takes such pleasure in regaling us with the daily dirt, but you just happen to be today's main scoop."

"Me? What on earth are you talking about? There isn't a darn thing about me that's interesting to the people who read that rag."

"Well, you may think that, but your troubles with the Dixons seem to be newsworthy enough to get you a mention right at the top of the page."

Liddy Lou closed her eyes, pinched the bridge of her nose, and pulled in a deep breath.

"Thank you for the heads-up, but I had a very long talking-to with myself yesterday and I've decided to put this in the good Lord's hands and let him sort this mess out before I muck it up any more than I already have."

Evie laughed. "Well then, I wish you luck, but I give it two days tops before you break another remote."

"Some best friend you are. I'm hanging up now. When you can be bothered to pull yourself away from today's paper I'll be waiting on the front porch for you to pick me up. And make it quick; I'm old and hungry."

Ten minutes after hanging up Liddy Lou stood waiting on the porch. She could hear Evie Newsome's side-by-side approaching down the access road that separated their properties. Liddy Lou laughed to herself thinking how ridiculous the two of them must look at their age, all gussied up and riding into town in a John Deer UTV.

The paved road into town went way out around River Front Park and took twice as long as the trail path through the woods but the latter was too rough for a car to travel.

As usual, Evie gave the side-by-side too much gas and overshot the turn into the front driveway of the Red Herring Inn, scaring Beecher's chickens and sending them running for cover.

She lurched to a stop at the bottom of the steps and hollered out, "All aboard who's coming aboard. Next stop, Castle Creek Diner."

Liddy Lou hustled down the stairs and had barely gotten herself into the seat when Evie tromped the gas and peeled out of the driveway, sending chickens running and squawking all over the place again.

Liddy Lou kept one hand on the roll bar and one on her hat as Evie careened down the dirt path dodging pot holes and low-hanging branches. As they approached the end of the path, Evie laid on the horn to let pedestrians know that they were about to enter the intersection where the path crossed over the sidewalk of Main Street. Evie popped the curb so hard it lifted them both a few inches off the seat. A young couple with a double stroller was gawking at them like they were driving down the street on fire, and Liddy Lou couldn't help laughing out loud as Evie let out a big "Whoop!"

They might be old country girls, but they still knew how to tear it up, she thought to herself.

Evie wheeled the muddy, green side-by-side into an open spot in front of the Castle Creek Diner and turned to look at Liddy Lou. "Your hat's crooked; might wanna address that before we head in."

"Well, I can't imagine how that happened with you being such a cautious driver."

"You should consider yourself lucky it was me driving and not Putt. He drives like a little old lady. We'd a starved before he got us here."

Liddy Lou kept her comments to herself as she adjusted her hat and smoothed her crushed velvet blazer. She'd been best friends with Evie Newsome since they'd been girls. When it came to Evie's husband, Putt, Liddy Lou tolerated him out of respect for Evie, but he was like a hangover from a two-dollar bottle of wine, cheap and miserable.

As they exited the side-by-side, Liddy Lou noticed Hilde Sanders blabbing away to Carol Besom and Molly Clausen just outside the entrance to the diner. They were pretending not to notice Evie and Liddy Lou approaching, which immediately signaled to Liddy Lou that they were being gossiped about—after all, that's what Hilde did best, and often.

Evie slowed to a stop and placed a hand on Liddy Lou's forearm. "Do you want to go somewhere else?" she asked.

"Certainly not. Hilde Sanders and her brood of gossip hens can talk all they want but they cannot talk another hole in my ass."

Evie gasped then started giggling uncontrollably.

"Liddy Lou Cormier, you are incorrigible, and I would be more than glad to get back in the side-by-side and open a path to that front door if this is where you want to eat."

The hen party broke up as they reached the door. Carol and Molly darted away with a muttered hello, but Hilde bounded up to them like she had tiny trampolines in her Birkenstocks.

"Howdy, ladies. Stopping in for some lunch?" Hilde didn't even give them time to answer before she laid into Liddy Lou. "So, Liddy Lou, you know I'm not one to spread rumors…"

Liddy Lou flinched and stifled a yelp as Evie dug her bony fingers into her arm. She wondered to herself why people with terrible habits always felt it necessary to start sentences by telling you they aren't one to do whatever it was they were about to do.

Liddy Lou plastered on a smile hoping it didn't look too forced. She swatted at Evie's hand, and Evie unlocked her fingers from Liddy Lou's forearm. Liddy Lou stepped forward, planted herself squarely in front of Hilde, and locked eyes with her.

"Save your bile for someone else, Hilde. I'm already aware Spenser Penn had the poor taste to make my publishing issues the topic of the day. No, I do not wish to discuss it, and I would really appreciate it if you could just this once restrain yourself from stirring it up with everyone in the county."

Hilde looked wounded, as if Liddy Lou had just accused her of skimming cash from the collection plate. She placed a hand over her heart and feigned innocence.

"Liddy Lou, I certainly wouldn't do anything so hurtful as to spread malicious gossip about a friend—which by the way, I've always considered us to be. I was just hoping to hear your side, is all. Everyone knows you cannot trust half of what you read in

Spenser's column. He takes the tiniest bit of hearsay and sensationalizes it to sell more papers."

Evie had remained quiet throughout this whole exchange but sensed that Liddy Lou was near her breaking point and intervened.

"Hilde, dear, it's been lovely chatting with you, but we're famished, and we're going to head in now. I'm sure we'll chat again soon."

Evie placed her hand on Liddy Lou's back and gave her a gentle shove towards the door.

Hilde was about to start yammering away again when the door opened, and Sheriff Andy Hansen emerged. He removed his hat and took turns kissing Evie and Liddy Lou's hands.

"Ladies, always lovely to see the two of you. Have yourselves a wonderful lunch."

Liddy Lou leaned forward and whispered, "I hope you saved room for dessert, because I happen to know there's a lemon cream tart and a delightful young lady at the Red Herring Inn who'd love you to stop by this afternoon for coffee." Andy released her and smiled shyly.

"Well, thank you for the tip. I'll be sure to follow up on that promptly."

He stepped back and pulled open the door, giving Liddy Lou and Evie a much-needed window of opportunity to escape Hilde Sanders.

Chapter 9

When Liddy Lou and Evie entered the diner, it was hard to ignore the stares and whispers, yet there were still a few people in Castle Creek on Liddy Lou's side. One of them happened to be the Junior League president, Tess Nichols. Tess was sitting near the window with Maggie Lorson and Ann Marie White.

"Yoo-hoo, ladies, over here," she called, waving a polka dotted handkerchief around like she was attempting to surrender to a conquering army.

Evie looked at Liddy Lou and shrugged her shoulders.

"Hope your plan wasn't to slip in unannounced and have a quiet, casual brunch. Anyone who didn't notice us when we first walked in is now aware we're here."

"Good, let 'em get it all out of their systems at once, and then we can all just put this whole mess behind us."

Evie cast a sideways glance at Liddy Lou. "Do you really mean that or are you just trying to be civil?"

Liddy Lou laughed and patted her best friend on the shoulder.

"Hell, no, I don't mean that, and these petty scandalmongers had better keep their distance, or I just might have to tell the whole bunch of 'em what I really think."

As they made their way to the table, Dot Hendricks swooshed by with a fully loaded tray of food in one hand and a pot of coffee in the other.

"Hey, gals. Grab a seat. I'll be over to take your order in three flicks of a coon's tail."

"Good Lord, where does she come up with some of her sayings?" Evie asked with a chuckle as they reached the table to join their friends.

As promised, Dot reappeared quickly to take their orders. "Ladies, how y'all doing today? Today's special is the..." Dot paused for effect, "same damn special we've been offering for the last twenty years. Okay, now that we've covered the formalities, who's coming to book club this week? It's Laura Gibson's turn to bring the main snack, and I'm gonna need at least a few of you ladies to cover me while I probe it for stray cat hairs."

The table erupted in giggles and at least one snort from Maggie Lorson.

"Oh, come on, now, Dot, Laura only has a handful of cats. How bad can it be?" Maggie teased.

"A handful? Last I knew she had six, which is five too many if you ask me."

Dot wriggled her whole body like a dog shaking off the rain.

"Now, let's get back to business. Everyone having their usual?"

The ladies ate their food at a leisurely pace and savored their mimosas. Maggie asked Liddy Lou how things were progressing with her nephew Andy and Liddy Lou's granddaughter Q'Bita, and they all enjoyed Evie's retelling of Putt's run-in with a rather aggressive nest of hornets. They were just about to finish up their main course when the front door opened, and Macie Dixon and her entourage flocked into the diner.

Macie looked in their direction and then scanned the diner before returning her attention to their table. She flagged Dot over with her best pageant wave, and they appeared to be having a conversation that wasn't pleasing either of them. Dot was shaking her head side to side in obvious disagreement, but Macie didn't seem to be relenting.

Dot slapped the coffee pot down on the counter and marched towards their table.

"Ladies, Ms. Dixon has requested that I ask you to relocate to another table. It seems this table has the best sun light and it stimulates her creative mojo. I, of course, told her no, but she's insisting that I at least ask."

Dot lowered her voice and leaned in across the table, "So help me Jesus, if one of you even considers getting up from this table I'll spit in your coffee every day for a week." Dot straightened herself upright. "Okay, then. I asked but I certainly understand why you're not willing to move to another table. I'll just let Ms. Dixon know that she can either take what we have available or wait until this one becomes open."

Dot turned and practically skipped back to where Macie stood waiting for a reply.

The whole table was glued to the conversation taking place near the front of the diner. Dot had just delivered the bad news, and Macie was turning purple and having a tantrum. One of Macie's entourage, a petite girl with oversized round glasses and long, brown hair, kept putting a hand on Macie's shoulder to calm her down but Macie kept swatting at her hand and finally pushed her away. By this time Macie had made such a scene the whole diner was watching to see what would happen next. Dot finally shrugged her shoulders in frustration and turned to walk away.

"Come back here this instant!" Macie snapped as Dot retreated to the kitchen. When Dot failed to even acknowledge her, Macie rounded on the petite girl who'd tried to defuse the situation.

"This is unacceptable! This is just one more example of your incompetence, Hadleigh. You know I always sit at that table for these meetings. You knew we were coming here today, so why would you not call ahead and have them reserve MY table?"

"Dear God, Macie, please lower your voice. This is not the Castle Creek Country Club. They do not take reservations here."

Macie's eyes were now just two small dark slits in her face. Her nostrils were flaring, and she was taking shallow, rapid breaths. Macie's words came out like venom.

"I do not want to hear your pathetic excuses, Hadleigh. I want that table, and I want it now, so go redeem yourself and explain to them why they will be moving to another table."

Liddy Lou was surprised the tiny girl could look even smaller, but she seemed to melt a little as Macie snapped at her.

"Go. Now."

Macie pointed in the direction of their table.

As Hadleigh made her way towards their table, Liddy Lou could see the tears welling in her big, brown eyes. She stopped a foot or two back from their table and barely made eye contact, her voice but a whisper.

"Hello, ladies. I'm sorry to disturb you. I'm Hadleigh Banks, Macie Dixon's assistant."

The group murmured in simultaneous greeting. Hadleigh was shaking like a frightened dog. Liddy Lou felt sorry for her, but no matter how sweet or mistreated this poor girl was, she had no intention of leaving her chair, even at the risk of becoming incontinent.

"I know the waitress has already asked nicely but I was hoping if I made a personal plea you might reconsider switching tables."

The last few words came out came out like the squeak of a mouse.

Liddy Lou removed the napkin from her lap and dabbed at the corners of her mouth, then folded the napkin and laid it down on the table. The rest of the table was holding their breath, afraid to be the first to speak.

Liddy Lou glanced around the table and then spoke in a low but stern voice.

"Young lady, you seem quite sweet despite your poor choice in employer. I'm not sure if you know who I am but I can assure you that I am the last person on earth who would vacate my seat for the likes of Macie Dixon."

The rest of the table was a choir of agreement, and Hadleigh acquired the pained look of someone who knows they're defeated but is being compelled by some unseen force to keep trying.

"Ma'am, you're right, I don't know who you are, and for that I apologize, but if you'd just hear me out," Hadleigh pleaded.

Much to Liddy Lou's relief, Tess finally found her voice.

"Miss... um... Banks, was it?"

Hadleigh nodded and gave Tess a hopeful half-smile.

"I don't want to make things any worse for you, because it's obvious that even the dead could have heard the dressing-down Macie gave you before you came over here, but even she can't be so thick as to think anyone at this table would show her the least bit of courtesy after what she's done to Liddy Lou."

Tess extended her hand in Liddy Lou's direction as she spoke, and a sudden look of understanding washed across Hadleigh's face.

"Oh, Dear God, you're Liddy Lou Cormier?" Hadleigh said as all the color drained from her face.

Before Liddy Lou could answer, Macie appeared at Hadleigh's side. She didn't even bother acknowledging the ladies at the table.

"Hadleigh, what the hell is taking so long? This is unacceptable. Get that waitress back over here to clear this table and tell her to bring me sparkling water, room temperature, not cold, and the glass'd better be clean."

Evie looked at her lunch companions and muttered, "Guess she really don't know much about food otherwise she'd know honey gets you further than vinegar."

Macie's head snapped around like she was being exorcised. "I heard that, Evie! You need to shut your pie hole and mind your own business, you crazy old shrew."

Before Macie's words could even fully register with the rest of the table, Liddy Lou shot out of her chair and shoved a finger in Macie's face.

"Now you look here, you spoiled, ungrateful, miserable child. You may have gotten away with stealing my recipes and ruining the launch of my book, but you will not disrespect my best friend."

Liddy Lou's voice was loud enough it carried throughout the whole restaurant.

Macie's mouth was hanging open so wide she could have swallowed a chicken whole. Her voice was as shrill and grating as nails on a chalkboard.

"You have no proof that I've done anything wrong. If you did, your publisher would have put up a fight. You also cannot attack me in public. My father has a battalion of lawyers, and they're going to have a field day with this." Macie crossed her arms, tapped her foot, and stared at Liddy Lou with a petulant smirk on her face.

Liddy Lou felt something inside her snap, and she couldn't control herself as she reached out with both hands and gave Macie Dixon a shove, sending her to the floor, rump first.

Maggie Lorson let out another snort, and Tess Nichols almost overturned the table trying to get out of her seat. She quickly put herself between Liddy Lou and Macie.

"Okay, ladies, let's just calm down."

Macie got back to her feet and was looking wildly around the diner.

"Please tell me someone got that on video. Hadleigh, call the sheriff and then call my father and tell him to have his lawyers here ASAP. I'm pressing charges and I don't want those idiots at the Castle Creek Sheriff's Department to mess up the investigation."

Liddy Lou chortled like a horse and stepped around Tess Nichols.

"Pressing charges? For what, performing a long overdue public service?"

"You just assaulted me, you ridiculous cow."

This time Evie got to her feet to give Tess some back-up. "Listen to me, Liddy Lou Cormier, you need to cool down and ignore this wretched child. Everything you've said is true, and your real friends know that, but she also has a rich daddy who has more pull than common decency. I don't want to have to bail you out of jail."

Normally Evie could talk Liddy Lou off the highest ledge, but Macie Dixon had hit a nerve and Liddy Lou wasn't going to let her have the last word.

"Thank you for your concern, Evie, but if I were you I'd keep that bail money handy because one of these days soon Miss Macie's mouth is going to push me a duck's feather too far and I'm going to shut it for her permanently."

Macie's face turned so red it looked like she'd been slapped.

"Are you threatening me with physical harm now, Liddy Lou?"

"You can take my comments any way you want, just like you took my recipes."

Liddy Lou grabbed her purse and headed for the register as every eye in the restaurant turned to watch her. Dot stood next to the register. She held up both her hands as Liddy Lou approached.

"Oh, don't you worry about the check, darling. Today's meal is on the house. Yours too, Evie."

When they reached the side-by-side Evie felt it might finally be safe to speak.

"Okay, now this is coming from a place of love because you are my oldest and dearest friend."

Liddy Lou held up a hand to stop her.

"If you're going to tell me that I shouldn't have lost my temper, you're wrong. She had that coming. If you're going to tell me that I took things a little too far and I've probably just made things way worse, well I know that. Am I upset with myself? I should be, but honestly, I'm not. It felt damn good to knock that little fraud on her backside, and my only regret is that it was a shove and not a sucker punch."

The side-by-side growled to life as Evie turned the key and punched the gas.

"Okay then, good talk."

Chapter 10

Q'Bita stood in the middle of the kitchen herb garden watching a pair of iridescent dragonflies chase each other in a dizzying mating dance. The sun felt warm on her skin but not so warm as to make it unpleasant to be in the garden. She bent down and plucked a few sprigs of Cuban mojito mint to steep in simple syrup that would later become a glaze for coconut lime muffins, the main attraction of this afternoon's tea service. She gently tousled the top of the large chocolate mint plant and inhaled deeply, savoring the smell that reminded her of mint chocolate chip ice cream. While she was there, she decided to grab a few sprigs of pineapple mint that she could chiffonade and pair with fresh berries and cream.

The entire grounds of the Red Herring Inn were beautiful, but the kitchen herb garden held a special place in Q'Bita's heart. When she and her husband Alain had moved from Paris to the countryside of Spain, Alain surprised her by having a landscape architect design and plant a kitchen herb garden a few steps out the back door of Q'Bita's bistro. After Alain's death, Q'Bita had sold her restaurant and returned to the States to be at the Red Herring with her family. The kitchen herb garden here, a gift from her brother Beecher and his husband Rene, reminded her of her garden in Spain. It gave her such peace to spend time here.

Q'Bita heard a rustling sound coming from the tall patch of lavender at the far end of the garden and realized she wasn't alone. Always wary of critters like skunks and snakes, she exited to the side of the garden, made a wide semi-circle around the outside edge, and approach the lavender patch from behind.

As she inched closer with slow, quiet steps, the rustling grew louder, and she could see the lavender stalks swaying, their floral sweetness perfuming the air at this end of the garden. She couldn't tell what had taken up residence among the thick patch, but it seemed big and, so far, unaware she was approaching.

Q'Bita reached the edge of the garden and paused for a few seconds before leaning in for a closer look. A sudden movement caught her off guard as a small bird shot out of the lavender followed by something huge that leapt at Q'Bita, hitting her right smack in the chest and knocking her backwards to the ground. She panicked for a few seconds as the breath returned to her body, but soon realized her attacker was rubbing its over-sized, furry head against her chin and purring like an earthquake on her chest.

Q'Bita reached up with a gloved hand and scratched Rolfie between the ears.

"Hello, beautiful. Sorry if I interrupted your hunt."

Rolfie stopped rubbing and moved up her chest so he was looking directly into Q'Bita's face. He let out a small yowl of forgiveness and hopped off, prancing away to continue his search for a fresh kill.

Q'Bita was still lying in the warm grass recovering from her encounter with Rolfie when she heard the crunch of gravel as a car entered the driveway. She pushed up on one elbow to see who'd arrived. A rush of excitement flooded through her as she noticed the words Castle Creek Sheriff Department on the side of the SUV.

Andy Hansen unfolded himself from the driver's seat and started towards her.

"Q'Bita, are you okay?"

She'd been so excited to see him she'd completely forgotten she was still laying in the grass beside the garden. She stood up and tried to brush away the muddy paw prints from the front of her apron.

"Oh, I'm fine. Just had a small run-in with Beecher and Rene's cat. I lost, in case you couldn't tell."

Andy laughed. "Yeah, sorry to say but I think he might have gotten the best of you. He's a big boy, that one. He managed to traipse over to the Pearson place last week, and Connie called us all worked up, claiming a puma was terrorizing her chickens. Can't say my deputies were all that impressed when they got there and found Rolfie instead of a puma."

Q'Bita removed her gardening gloves and stooped to pick her herb basket. Andy bent down and helped her gather the last of the spilled herbs. They were close enough she could smell his musky cologne and see a small bead of sweat snaking its way beneath the collar of his uniform shirt. They locked gazes, and Q'Bita wondered what it would be like to just lay there in the warm grass kissing his neck and being held in his arms.

A symphony of squawking and the flapping of wings from the edge of the driveway drew her back to reality. Rolfie had evidently found the chickens.

Andy smiled at her and extended his hand to help her up. Q'Bita took his hand and pulled herself closer to the handsome sheriff.

"Let's get you inside before we end up on Rolfie's menu. I have something I think you might like."

"I just bet you do," Andy said playfully. "Word on the street has it that you might have a fresh lemon cream tart in there."

"Word on the street, you say? Just who have you been talking to?"

"I had the pleasure of running into your nana and Evie Newsome at the diner this morning. Liddy Lou suggested I stop by and offered up the lemon cream tart as bait. Not that I need any extra motivation to stop by and see you, though."

"Nice recovery, Sheriff, but just know that if lemon cream tart is what it takes to have you stop by for a visit, I'll make one seven days a week."

Q'Bita threaded her arm through the crook of Andy's elbow and steered him towards the side door to the kitchen. A small twinge of guilt bubbled to the surface as she turned to glance back at the kitchen herb garden. She had loved Alain, but even in the beginning of their relationship, he never gave her the kind of butterflies she got when she was close to Andy Hansen.

35

As they entered the kitchen, the buttery, yeasty smell of baking bread wrapped them in its embrace.

"Man, I love the way this place smells. How do you keep so slim, Q'Bita? If I lived here I'd look like Rolfie's twin."

A familiar voice from near the walk-in said, "No, you wouldn't. I'm pretty sure he'd eat you before he accepted you as his equal. It's survival of the fattest with that one."

Tom Block emerged from the walk-in with a tray containing a crock of French butter, four hard-boiled eggs, a stick of Beecher's homemade salami, and a small assortment of cheeses. He sat the tray down on the counter and shook Andy's hand.

"Sheriff Hansen, always nice to see you. Hope this is a social call and not official business."

"Semi-official, actually. One of my informants told me that your daughter had a stash of lemon cream tarts and I had to investigate to make sure this wasn't a case of possession without intent to distribute."

The crime writer in Tom appreciated a good legal play on words so he couldn't help laughing.

"Well then, if you'll excuse me, I'll just grab my baguette out of the warming oven and let you get on with your investigation."

Q'Bita tore a big sheet of bee's wax parchment paper from the roll hanging beneath the spice cabinet and placed it on the counter. She removed the toasty baguette from the warming drawer, laid it in the center of the parchment, and skillfully wrapped it so just the corner of the loaf was exposed. She handed it to her father and gave him a peck on the cheek.

"Don't forget the wine. It wouldn't be a proper picnic without wine."

"Oh, that's your mother's job. She's the wine snob in this marriage. I'm more of a bourbon man myself."

Andy's ears perked up at the mention of bourbon.

"Heck, Tom, I didn't know you were a bourbon lover. My pappy makes some of the best bourbon in these parts. He's just about ready to do a tasting of a new sweet mash he's been perfecting. If you're up for it and don't mind a little cigar smoke, you'd be more than welcome to join us Saturday night. We're going to do a tasting during our weekly poker game."

Tom was grinning like a little kid on Christmas morning. "I'd love to. I haven't had a guy's night out in forever."

Q'Bita felt another little pang of guilt pass through her. She loved that Andy and her family had a good relationship. Alain had never been close to them. She tried to tell herself it was the distance that kept them at arm's length, but truth be told, Alain just didn't have any interest in forming a relationship with them. His interest was Q'Bita, and that was as far as it extended.

As she stood watching the two of them make their plans, it occurred to her that while she'd loved her time spent living in Europe, she'd never been as content as she was right here, right now, in tiny, rural Castle Creek, West Virginia.

After her father said his goodbyes and left the kitchen, Andy gave Q'Bita a sheepish look.

"Sorry. I guess I should have asked first. Are you're okay with me inviting your dad to hang out?"

"Oh, absolutely. Beecher is going on a hunting trip this weekend, and if dad is hanging out with you, that gives Mom, Rene, Nana, and I a chance to put together some welcome baskets for the guests. Nana's been pretty upset about everything going on with the book, and it would do her some good to have a girl's baking and crafting night."

"Yeah, I didn't want to mention it earlier but when I ran into Liddy Lou and Evie at the diner it looked like your nana was having a pretty heated discussion with Hilde Sanders. I imagine Spenser Penn's column in today's paper may have had a thing or two to do with that."

"You read the gossip page? I pegged you more as a sports page or comics kind of guy."

Andy sat down while Q'Bita poured them each a glass of sweet tea. His hand brushed hers as he reached for the glass. His fingertips gently stroked the back of her hand as she sat the glass down in front of him. He looked at her and smiled. They were both wrapped up in the moment until Q'Bita's mom entered the kitchen.

"Sorry to interrupt, kids. I'll just be a second. Tom forgot the honey and the apricots."

Andy stood to greet Kari.

"Mrs. Block. Always a pleasure to see you. This must be my lucky day, getting to see all three of the lovely ladies in this family."

Kari blushed. "That's sweet of you to say, Andy, but there's no reason to be so formal. You can call me Kari. And I'd say it's the ladies of this family that are lucky to see you. So polite and handsome."

Kari reached out and squeezed his bicep. Q'Bita turned scarlet with embarrassment.

"Excuse my mother. She's a closeted romance writer and hopeless flirt."

Kari gave her daughter a hug and kissed her cheek.

"I am not closeted. If anyone were to ever connect me to those books, I'd admit I wrote them even if they are complete smutty drivel. I was young and horny, but at least I had the good sense to act out my fantasies on the page instead of in person. Well, at least until your father came along, that is."

"Oh my God, Mom, I can't believe we're having this conversation in front of Andy. Why don't I grab those apricots while you grab the honey, so you can get back to your picnic?"

Andy had clearly sensed Q'Bita was feeling uncomfortable, and the devil in him couldn't resist turning up the heat a bit.

"So, Mrs. Block... I mean, Kari. Those smutty books still in print? I've been meaning to expand my reading list."

His question had come out so lasciviously that Q'Bita felt flush with heat just thinking about Andy reading her Mother's books.

As Kari reached the swinging doors to the dining room, she glanced back at Andy and Q'Bita with a wicked smile.

"I'll be sure to have Q'Bita stop by with a full set of autographed copies. FYI, they're a very erotic couple's read if you're into that kind of thing."

Before Q'Bita could scold her, Kari bumped the doors open with her hip and slipped out of the kitchen.

Andy turned to look at Q'Bita. Her mouth was still hanging open and she was sure she was the color of a boiled lobster. He looked like he felt bad for her, but the twinkle in his eye told her he also enjoyed knowing that the thought of the two of them reading steamy sex scenes evoked such a reaction.

"I am so sorry," Q'Bita sputtered. "We were talking about something before my mother came in."

"You're right, we were, but I'd much rather talk about you bringing me those books."

Q'Bita let out the breath she'd been holding since her mother had left the kitchen and shook her head.

"Andy Hansen, you're as terrible as she is. Now quit distracting me and get back to our conversation about Spenser's column."

"Oh, right. It was the main topic of conversation at the diner thanks to Hilde Sanders, so I doubt Liddy Lou and Evie are going to enjoy their brunch much."

A look of concern flashed across Q'Bita's face.

"Oh Lord. Well, this isn't good. Nana has let this whole mess upset her to the point she might just explode if someone pushes the subject with her. I can't believe the Castle Creek Gazette would even let Spenser publish such lies."

Andy nodded in agreement.

"This is a small town and people here love a good scandal even if it's not the least bit true. They also love to spread gossip like wild fire, sometimes to the point the situation boils over, which is exactly why I read the gossip column. It comes in handy to know who's feuding with whom, or is accused of what, if it gets out of hand and my deputies and I need to sort it all out. Spenser's column is also how I found out my own deputy is planning to run against me the next election."

Q'Bita stood up and moved towards the walk-in.

"Well, now that we've established you have a valid reason for reading the gossip page, how about I get you some of that lemon cream tart? And for the record, Chance Holleran can waste his time and money running against you if he wants, but most of the people in this town respect and admire you so there's no way he'll win."

Andy laughed.

"I take it I have your vote, at least? Now, enough with the gossip. I want to get back to hearing about your mom's books."

Q'Bita felt the butterflies return, and for just a minute she let herself wonder what it would be like to lay in bed next to Andy and act out some of the steamier scenes from her mother's books.

Chapter 11

Andy was half-way through his second helping of lemon cream tart, and Q'Bita had just put on a fresh pot of coffee, when Andy's cell phone buzzed with an incoming text.

"That's weird. It's Chance. I wonder why he didn't just call. Texting isn't really his thing."

Andy swiped a finger across the screen and opened the text. "You alone?"

Andy tapped in his reply.

"Depends. If your next question is what I am wearing, I can promise your performance review is going to be pretty awkward this year."

Chance replied quickly.

"You're not funny, Andy. We have a situation that might be even more awkward than my review. If you're still with the girlfriend, you might want to find somewhere private and give me a call at the station."

Q'Bita had returned to the counter and was waiting for Andy to finish.

"Everything okay?"

"Not sure. He needs me to give him a call. I'm just going to step outside and see what's up."

Andy walked to the far end of the driveway before calling the station. Chance picked on the first ring.

"Hey, Andy. Can any of the Blocks hear you?"

"No, I'm outside. What's up?"

Andy could hear Chance fidgeting in his seat.

"Well, I just got a call from Red Dixon, and he's pissing fire. Seems Macie and Liddy Lou Cormier had a minor altercation at the

Castle Creek Diner today, and Red claims Miss Liddy Lou assaulted Macie. He's headed down here with his pack of legal hyenas, and he's insisting we arrest Miss Liddy Lou and charge her with a whole wheelbarrow of offenses. Thought you might want to get back here and get this mess under control before things blow up any further."

Andy kicked at the stones in the driveway.

"Son of a bitch! You have to be kidding me. Liddy Lou Cormier is almost eighty years old. Does Red Dixon really think she has it in her to assault anyone? This is just asinine."

Chance let out a chuckle.

"I wouldn't be so sure of yourself, Andy. Rumor has it Miss Liddy Lou got the best of Macie. Man, I wish I'd been there to see it go down."

"For God's sake, Chance, grow up. I'll be there in ten minutes, and no one is to go near Liddy Lou Cormier until I get to the bottom of this, you hear me?"

Andy ended his call and looked back at the Red Herring Inn trying to decide what if anything he should tell Q'Bita. He couldn't just leave without saying anything, but he also didn't want to get her or her family all upset until he knew for sure what was going on.

Before he could decide, Q'Bita opened the kitchen door and came outside. She was scattering hunks a bread around the driveway when she caught sight of Andy.

"Oh, you're done. Everything okay?"

Andy massaged the skin just above his eyebrows and then rubbed his hand down his face while he pondered what to say. He crossed the driveway, closing the distance between them.

"I'm sorry, sweetheart, but something's come up and I'm afraid I'm gonna have to take a raincheck on that coffee."

He hesitated and Q'Bita asked, "Nothing serious, I hope?"

Andy kicked at the stones on the driveway with the toe of his boot, and it made a crunching sound. He glanced up at Q'Bita, who was now standing with both hands on her hips, giving him a look that said she wasn't going to just let this drop.

"Okay. Out with it, mister. What aren't you telling me?"

Andy moved a few steps closer and put his hands on Q'Bita's shoulders.

"I'll tell you what's up, but you have to promise to just stay calm and let me do my job. You have my word I'll get to the bottom of this as quick as possible."

Q'Bita made an audible gulping noise and looked up at Andy. "If you have to ask me to stay calm, then we both know that there is very little likelihood I will. If there's something wrong, you need to tell me straight out."

Andy removed his hands, shoving them in his pockets, and took a step back.

"It appears your nana and Macie Dixon may have had a bit of a row at the diner, and now Red Dixon has his boxer shorts all in a bunch about it. Chance says he's on his way to the station with his legal guys and wants to press charges."

Q'Bita's rosy glow from earlier had now changed to a ghostly pale, and her voice cracked with emotion when she spoke.

"Charges? Against my nana? But Andy, can they even do that for some silly bickering back and forth?"

Andy felt the skin on the back of his neck and ears starting to burn. He hated seeing Q'Bita upset.

"According to what Red said when he spoke to Chance, it sounds like things might have gotten physical between them."

Q'Bita's fear was instantly replaced with anger.

"Physical? You mean to tell me Macie Dixon put her hands on my nana? My nana wouldn't hurt a fly. If that wretched brat did anything to hurt my nana the Dixons had better hope they have the best lawyers in all of West Virginia, because I've had enough of those people to last me a lifetime, and I'll make sure Nana sues them for every penny they've got."

Andy ran his hand down the length of his face again and rubbed at the rough stubble on his chin.

"Actually, Q'Bita, as much as I can't believe it, it sounds like Liddy Lou may have been the aggressor. I wasn't there, so right now all I have is one set of people's words against another. You know I care about you and I adore your nana, but I have an obligation as sheriff to hear everyone out and to get to the bottom of what really happened. I promise you I'll keep an open mind and won't let anyone press charges until I find out what really happened."

Andy felt a tightness in his chest as he saw a tear roll down Q'Bita's cheek. There was a tiny tremble in her lower lip, and she bit down hard to try and hide it.

"Andy, promise me you'll handle this, not your deputies. Most people in this town are afraid of upsetting Red and let the Dixons do their thinking for them, and it's not fair. They've done enough damage to Nana already. They shouldn't get away with anything more."

"You have my word. I'd better get down there before Red Dixon has my whole station riled up."

Andy reached out and pulled Q'Bita close. She sunk into his chest and hugged him tightly. He could feel her tiny frame shaking and it was melting his resolve. He knew he shouldn't let his personal relationships impact his work, but he had feelings for Q'Bita he'd never had for any other woman, and he couldn't help himself.

"Would it make you feel better if you came with me?"

He knew it was a terrible idea as soon as the words came out, but it was too late to take them back now.

Q'Bita stood on her tiptoes and kissed his cheek.

"Give me two seconds to shut off the coffee pot and grab my purse."

She turned and started jogging towards the kitchen door, but she stopped and turned towards him.

"Thanks, Andy. This means more to me than you can imagine." She smiled at him, and for the moment he didn't care if he'd done the right thing or not.

Chapter 12

The lobby of the Castle Creek Sheriff's Office was too small to hold Red Dixon and his assorted lawyers. It was getting warm and Red was getting impatient. Maggie Lorson hoped he had the poor judgment to start complaining. She'd personally see to it their paperwork got tied up till every cow in Castle Creek came home.

Red Dixon approached her desk and she pretended not to notice him. He cleared his throat and leaned forward, resting both hands on her desk.

"Damn it, Maggie, don't pretend you don't know I'm standing here. When is your nephew going to get here? If he can't be bothered to do his job, I'll march back there and have Chance Holleran do it for him."

Maggie looked up at Red Dixon and blinked twice.

"I'm aware you're there. I just don't care. You do not intimidate me, Red Dixon, so just park yourself over there and wait for the sheriff to get back."

Red banged his fist on the edge of Maggie's desk.

"You won't be so flippant this fall when I put all my financial resources and personal network behind Chance Holleran's run for sheriff. My taxes pay your salary and your nephew's salary, and I carry a lot of pull in this town."

Maggie threw Red a bored look, motioned to the lobby with her pen, and said, "Sit!"

Red threw up his hands in frustration and turned to one of his attorneys.

"Why are you all just standing around looking confused? Can't you do something?"

A deep voice cut through Red's complaining.

"Mr. Dixon, sorry to keep you waiting. Why don't you and your people follow me and see if we can't get this all worked out."

Andy turned to lead the group to his office and made it about two steps before Macie Dixon started squawking.

"Get this sorted out? Daddy, tell him we're not here to sort things out, we're here to have Liddy Lou Cormier arrested, and before she attacks me again."

Maggie's chair shot back with an ear-piercing scrap across the floor.

"Now you just hold on a minute. You started this whole thing by making a spectacle out of yourself and being rude."

Macie launched herself towards Maggie.

"You shut your mouth and stay out of this, Maggie."

The sound of laughter from the hallway drew everyone's attention. Chance Holleran and Mike Collins were leaning against opposite walls watching the circus unfolding.

Chance stepped forward and looked at his boss.

"Looks like you might need some help with crowd control, Andy. I can call in county SWAT if you think these folks are going to riot."

Andy scowled at his deputies.

"Don't be a smart-ass, Chance."

He turned to Maggie and shook his head in disgust.

"Please let me know if Liddy Lou Cormier or her attorney contacts us or comes in."

Maggie and Macie both started talking at the same time, until Andy held up a hand in their direction and raised his voice.

"Enough. I don't want to hear another word unless I direct a question to you. Are we clear?"

***

Q'Bita had been watching everything from an empty office just

46

down the hall from the lobby, staying hidden until Andy and the Dixons were settled in the big conference room next to Andy's office. Opening the door just a crack, she peaked out into the hallway to make sure the coast was clear. Then slipped out, closing the door behind her, and tiptoed to the lobby. She whispered Maggie's name, and Maggie almost fell out of her chair.

"My God, Q'Bita, where the hell did you come from? You scared the life out of me."

Q'Bita suppressed a small giggle.

"I'm sorry, Maggie. I came in the back with Andy and was hiding in the office around the corner. He thought it would be best if the Dixons didn't know he'd let me tag along."

Maggie shook her head, half in agreement, half in disgust. "Probably a good thing. They're out for blood and it wouldn't surprise me if they start questioning the impact of your relationship on Andy's objectivity. They're sneaky ones, I tell you. Too accustomed to everything going their way."

Q'Bita started biting her bottom lip again. She hadn't considered the impact their relationship might have on Andy's job.

"Maggie, you said you were there, at the diner. I can't believe Nana would just attack Macie Dixon for no reason. What really happened?"

"Oh, she had reason alright."

Q'Bita cringed as Maggie shared her version of events.

"Oh Lord, this isn't good. Red Dixon isn't going to let this go without making a fuss. Do you know where my nana is now?"

"Not sure. She and Evie left the diner right after it happened. Hopefully she's somewhere cooling off. I've known Liddy Lou for decades, and I've never seen her so angry, but I do have to say it was refreshing to see someone put Macie Dixon in her place for once."

Q'Bita excused herself and went outside to get some fresh air. She paced back and forth in front of the Castle Creek Sheriff's Station contemplating what to do next, and finally decided to call

Liddy Lou and give her a heads-up. The phone rang twice and went to voicemail, which wasn't a good sign. Liddy Lou was always forgetting where she put her phone and missing calls by the time she found it, so Jamie had adjusted it to ring several times before going to voicemail. Two rings then voicemail meant Liddy Lou had seen the call and sent Q'Bita to voicemail on purpose.

Q'Bita waited a minute, called again, and was sent to voicemail after just one ring this time.

"Nana, I know what you're doing, and sending me to voicemail isn't helping. You need to call me when you hear this. I'm at the Sheriff's Station, and the Dixons are here with enough lawyers to form a baseball team. They're trying to force Andy to charge you with assault and God knows what else. Please call me so we can figure out how to deal with this."

The sound of the front door opening drew Q'Bita's attention, and she turned to see the Dixons and their legal squad exiting the Sheriff's Station. She hung up the phone and shoved it in her back pocket.

Macie grabbed her father by the elbow and pointed at Q'Bita.

"What's she doing here?"

Macie let go of her father's arm and stomped up to Q'Bita, stopping inches from her face.

"If you think being Andy Hansen's whore is going to keep your nana from being arrested, you are sadly misinformed. Andy Hansen may be the law, but my father is the one with the real power in this town, and Liddy Lou is going to jail for what she did to me. That, I promise you."

Red extended his hands to his sides and titled his head upwards in a pleading gesture.

"Please, Muffin, give it a rest. Miss Block, if you and your family know what's good for you, I'd locate your grandmother and retain legal counsel as quickly as possible. The longer we drag this out the harder it's going to be on everyone. Well, everyone in your family, that is."

Red placed his hand on Macie's back and steered her towards the parking lot, his lawyers following close behind like a flock of baby ducks.

Chapter 13

With Macie occupied at the Sheriff's Station, Hadleigh decided to use the time to do some investigating. After being present for two conversations in the same week where the subject of stolen recipes had come up, she was determined to find out what Macie was hiding. Her first stop had been Macie's dressing room at the production studio, but that was a bust. Her next choice was Macie's home office at Dixon Manor.

The Dixons didn't call it that, but to Hadleigh, who grew up in a tiny apartment, the sprawling mansion sure felt that way.

Sometimes being Macie's assistant had its advantages; she could come and go on the Dixon estate and no one thought anything of it.

Hadleigh let herself into Macie's office and went straight for the big glass and chrome desk that occupied the center of the room. She checked each drawer but nothing interesting presented itself. Next, she stood behind the desk, slowly scanning the room for other places Macie might hide stolen recipes.

The office, like all the other rooms in Dixon Manor, was huge. Hadleigh loved the way Cookie, the current Mrs. Dixon, had decorated the estate. It had a welcoming, rustic country style, but unlike the rest of the Dixons' home, Macie's office had a sparse, urban loft vibe that didn't lend itself to many hiding places.

Hadleigh crossed the room and opened a set of double doors built into the wall. The inside was filled with shelves containing miscellaneous office supplies, printer paper, and binders full of paperwork related to The Macie Dixon Line.

As Hadleigh was putting the last of the binders back in place, she noticed a small button near the back of the shelf. It was painted to blend in and she had almost missed it. She pushed the button and heard a popping noise, then noticed the framed mirror next to the cabinet was now protruding about two inches outward from the wall.

Hadleigh closed the cabinet and moved closer to examine the mirror. She placed her hands on either side of the mirror and pulled gently. The mirror came free of the wall revealing a safe. Hadleigh sat the mirror on the floor and tugged on the handle but the safe was locked.

If there was one thing Hadleigh was certain of, it was Macie's narcissism, so she wasn't at all surprised when she tried Macie's birthday as the combination and the safe opened.

Hadleigh was shocked to find a stack of photocopied pages inside. Most of the pages were recipes, but some appeared to be stories and letters. Hadleigh leafed through the pages and found a few with note-filled margins, written in Macie's handwriting. Hadleigh also found a note stuck to one of the pages that read, "Now you owe me. Let me know when you're ready to settle up. T."

Hadleigh had been so absorbed in reading through the pages she hadn't heard anyone approaching the room. When the door opened, it startled her, and she dropped the stack of papers. She whirled around and saw Macie glowering at her.

Hadleigh stooped down and tried to pick up the pages that were now scattered about, but Macie was already on her. "What the hell are you doing in my office? How did you get that safe open?"

Macie gave her a shove and Hadleigh lost her balance, falling backwards onto the floor. Macie kicked the fallen papers across the floor as she advanced on Hadleigh.

"Answer me, Hadleigh. Did someone put you up to this? Liddy Lou Cormier and the Blocks have been trying to ruin me from the moment I began The Macie Dixon Line. Are you helping them? Did they pay you to spy on me?"

Macie loomed over her, screaming in Hadleigh's face, spittle flying as she over-emphasized every word of her tirade. Hadleigh did a little crab walk backwards and rose to her feet. If she was ever going to take her rightful place as a Dixon, she needed to stop letting Macie treat her like the help.

Hadleigh pushed her glasses back on her nose and did her best to look unfazed by Macie's hissy fit.

"Don't be so dramatic, Macie. No one put me up to anything, and no one is paying me to spy on you. I was just curious why everyone seems to think you stole recipes and why Liddy Lou Cormier is so angry with you. I figured this office is where I'd find the answers since you certainly wouldn't tell me the truth even if I asked."

One of the Dixons' maids opened the door and peered in.

"Is everything all right, Miss Macie?"

"We're fine, Angelique, and you need to learn to knock before entering my personal space," Macie snapped as she slammed the door closed in the maid's face.

Macie turned back to Hadleigh.

"Why would I need to share anything with you? You're my assistant, not my bestie. What's in this office is private and absolutely none of your business."

"Look, Macie, I think we both know exactly what those pages are and who they belong to. With that said, I have no intention of going down with you when the truth comes out, so I very much think it is my business."

The same flicker of fear Hadleigh saw the day the hot guy had shown up at the studio flashed across Macie's face, and Hadleigh knew she'd hit a nerve.

"You're a fraud, and I don't intend to get caught up in all this when it implodes."

Macie let out a derisive snort, and the look of fear was once again replaced with anger and self-righteous indignation.

"Hadleigh, do you know why I'm a successful entrepreneur and you're just an assistant? I'll tell you why. I have vision and the guts to do whatever it takes to succeed. You, on the other hand, waste time worrying about right and wrong. No one ever got anywhere worth being by playing fair. Fighting dirty is business 101, Hadleigh. That's how you succeed. Look around you. Do you think my father, or his father, got all this by playing fair? The Dixons are winners, Hadleigh. It's in our blood, and the Liddy Lou Cormiers of the world are not going to stop me from winning. I want the world to think of me when they hear the Dixon name, and I'll do whatever it takes to make The Macie Dixon Line the most successful lifestyle brand in the world. I'm the last in a long line of Dixons, and I have no intention of letting our winning streak end, so if you know what's good for you you'll keep your trap shut and do what I tell you to do."

This was the Macie that Hadleigh couldn't stand, the one who made her question how they could share a father and be so different. For Hadleigh, the next few minutes were like watching a train wreck unfold and being helpless to stop it. Anger took over, and words just came spilling out, words that once said couldn't be unsaid.

"Oh, spare me, Macie. You're not as successful as you like to tell everyone you are. You're a horrible person, and quite frankly your vision is as ridiculous and annoying as you are. You have a small handful of followers here in Castle Creek who flock to you so they can associate themselves with your family's name. For God's sake, your cooking show isn't even on a national station, and the only reason you have a show is because your father pays for it to be produced. The fact that you can't even come up with your own recipes and need to steal them from someone else is just sad and pathetic. It's no wonder half the people in this town mock you behind your back. If that's what it takes to be a winner and what it means to be a Dixon, then I'm glad our father didn't raise me."

Hadleigh hadn't intended for that last part to slip out but anger overrode her common sense.

The look on Macie's face was a mixture of hurt and confusion.

"What do you mean, our father?"

Hadleigh flopped down on the love seat and buried her face in her hands. This was bad, so bad, she thought to herself. How had she been so stupid? Macie was still standing by the safe, and Hadleigh could feel her watching her.

"Oh, I get it," Macie said. "You're another one of those scammers. You thought you could weasel your way into my life, get in my good graces, and I'd fall all over myself with excitement to have a long-lost sister. This is all a big game to get my father's money. Well, you're not the first scammer to target this family so you can just turn off the water works because your plan won't work."

Hadleigh wiped her cheeks with the back of her hand and sniffled.

"Macie, it's not a scam, it's true. I'm adopted, I've told you that before."

"Okay, so you're adopted. Big deal. That doesn't prove my father is your father. The only way you could prove that is with a paternity test, and my father would never agree to that."

"Actually, Macie, that's not the only way. By the time I hit my teens I wanted to know who my parents were and why they gave me up. My adopted parents tried going through the proper channels to find my birth parents but got nowhere. I was selfish and wouldn't let it drop, which led me to do some seriously stupid things that caused my parents a lot of heartache.

"My dad's brother, Brett, is a cop, and he tried to keep me out of trouble by bending the rules and running my DNA through the system to see if he could find a familial match that might lead to one of my parents. When the results came back there was a 99.996 percent match to your father."

"You're lying. My father is not a criminal, and there is no way his DNA is in some stupid database."

"Just because his DNA is on file doesn't make him a criminal, Macie. I have no idea why it was there, but my uncle Brett would have nothing to gain by lying about the DNA match."

"I don't care what the test says, Hadleigh. I'm only three months older than you so there's no way my parents could have had a second baby to give away. It's not physically possible."

Hadleigh rolled her eyes at Macie.

"It's possible if we share a father but have different mothers, Macie. I still don't know who my mother is, and honestly, that's the only thing I want from Red. I want to know who my mother is, and I want to hear her side of why she didn't keep me."

"Really, Hadleigh? Do you expect anyone to believe that story? It sounds ridiculous and would mean my father was cheating on my mother, which I very much doubt. What I don't doubt, though, is that you're a loser, and I have no tolerance for losers, so you're fired, but trust me, I plan to tell my father all about this little scam of yours. Once his lawyers are finished with you, you'll definitely regret the day you ever put your greedy little plan in place."

Hadleigh didn't bother defending herself to Macie. Once Macie's mind was made up there was no point trying to change it.

Soon, Red Dixon would either find out he had another daughter he didn't know existed or face the fact that a daughter he knew about, and chose to keep secret, was no longer secret.

Hadleigh was powerless to control what happened from here, and right now she wasn't sure she even cared. The Dixons were not the kind of family she wanted to be a part of anyway.

She got up from the love seat and started to leave the room without even looking at her half-sister. As she reached the doorway she stopped and said, "When I first found out about you I hoped we'd at least become friends someday. It's sad to me that you're so damaged you'll never know what it feels like to have a friend. I hope your success is enough for you, Macie."

55

Chapter 14

As the first slivers of daylight appeared outside her window, Q'Bita stretched and got out of bed. Beecher would be almost done feeding the animals, and she needed to start breakfast.

She dressed and headed for the kitchen. She could see the light shining under the door between the dining room and the kitchen. As she entered the kitchen, she was surprised to find her nana sitting at the counter, dabbing at her red, swollen eyes with a tissue.

"Nana! Are you okay?"

Liddy Lou sniffled and then blew her nose.

"Hello, baby. I'm sorry if all the commotion woke you. Rene was hysterical by the time they left, and I couldn't bring myself to shush him."

Q'Bita took a seat next to her nana and slid the tissue box a little closer.

"Oh God, what did I miss? Is someone hurt?"

"Oh, Q'Bita, I'm just heart-sick. When Beecher went out to feed his critters this morning Rolfie followed him to the barn. He got hold of some of my gopher bait. I'm not sure if he ate it or just inhaled it but he was having a horrible reaction. Beecher got some salted water into him and he started throwing up but there's no way to tell how much of the poison he ingested. It only takes the smallest amount to kill a coyote or even a person, for that matter. It wouldn't take much to kill a cat. Even one as big as Rolfie. I just hope they get him to the vet in time to counteract the poison."

"I'm sure Rolfie will be just fine, Nana." Q'Bita hoped her words came out sounding more hopeful than she felt inside.

"I hope you're right, baby. Rene will never forgive me if he isn't. He treats that cat like it's a child, and I can't imagine how devastated he'll be if the vet can't help."

Q'Bita got up and started making a fresh batch of biscuits. Her parents would be up soon and make their way to the kitchen. Biscuits were always best warm and consumed with fresh coffee. Cooking was how she coped with stress, and thankfully the rest of her family dealt with stress by eating. The rest of the morning dragged on at a painfully slow pace until Beecher finally called around eleven to say the vet was still treating Rolfie, but he'd be fine in a few days.

The sense of tension that had been hanging over everything finally lifted and Q'Bita was able to catch a few hours to herself. She pulled out her wedding book and flipped through the pages until she found the recipe for Comfort Casserole. Warm, bubbly, gooey comfort food was exactly what her family needed to set things right.

She made a quick shopping list and headed out the door. She called Evie and Jamie on her way into town and invited them to dinner. Evie offered to bring dessert and Q'Bita put Jamie in charge of wine.

Once she was finished shopping Q'Bita made a quick stop at Sammie Hake's flower shop to pick out some flowers for the table. Sammie's assistant rang up her purchase and was wrapping the flowers in paper just as Sammie came in from the back room. She smiled and waved.

"Hey, Q'Bita. This must be my lucky day, getting to see both my favorite customers. Liddy Lou stopped by earlier and picked up gift baskets and had me emboss more ribbon. I know I've probably said this before but I really do appreciate that you guys patronize the local merchants. It means a lot to little businesses like mine."

Q'Bita stayed and chatted for a few minutes then headed home to get dinner started.

Chapter 15

The production crew was getting antsy. Today's shoot should have started two hours ago, and there was still no sign of Macie or Hadleigh. Patti had shown up before the rest of the staff hoping to persuade Macie to wrap early so the crew could attend the Charleston Film Festival.

Prior to working on *Country Cooking With Macie,* three of the crew had filmed a documentary about waste and abuse in the restaurant industry, and their film was screening as the main event at the festival tonight.

Patti took one look at the cherry almond crumble she'd staged over an hour ago. It had not held up well under the hot lights of the set. She was just about to pull it off the counter when Macie finally made an appearance.

"Why are you all just standing around? This show doesn't stage and film itself. I'll be in my dressing room centering myself. You'd better be ready to roll when I walk back out here."

***

Macie walked down the hallway to her dressing room still reeling from the conversation with her father. How could he have kept all these secrets from her? It was like her whole life was a lie. Hadleigh was right, even her cooking show was a joke. The only part of her life that wasn't a farce was The Macie Dixon Line. The concept and designs were all hers, and it was something she was very proud of. She had an eye for color and a knack for knowing what looked good together, but these weren't skills that impressed someone like Red Dixon.

Red was all about money and building an empire, so right from the beginning Macie agreed to take on all the other pieces, like the cooking show, the blog, and the brand. She would much rather have focused on the product line until she'd perfected it, but her father drove her like she drove others, and she never wanted to come up short in his eyes.

She reached the door to her dressing room and noticed it was open a crack. She could hear someone moving around inside. Macie tiptoed to the door, peered in, and saw it was Hadleigh. She opened the door, and Hadleigh turned to look at her.

"Before you start screeching, Macie, I'm just here to get my personal things. You can check the box; I didn't steal anything."

Hadleigh motioned towards the copy-paper box sitting on the corner of Macie's desk.

Macie stepped inside and pulled the door partway shut behind her.

"No need to be so defensive, Hadleigh. I didn't accuse you of stealing anything."

"No, that's right. You accused me of being a scammer, a loser, and a liar but not a thief. Stealing is your flaw, not mine."

"Wow, and here I thought I was the only bitch in this family," Macie said sarcastically.

Hadleigh dropped the files she was holding into the box and stared at Macie.

"This family? So yesterday you accuse me of making this whole thing up to con your father out of his fortune and now we're family? Why the sudden change of heart, Macie?"

"Hadleigh, I know you won't believe this, but I'm not really as horrible as you think I am. I heard every word you said yesterday, and trust me, some of it stung. I called my father after you left and told him I needed to speak to him. When I told him about our conversation I expected him to react the same way I did, deny everything and call his lawyers, but he just went quiet. When he did finally say something, it was that his relationship with my mother was complicated, things weren't as perfect on the inside as they seemed on the outside, and they'd both done things to hurt the other. He insists he had no idea about you, and I believe him. And to prove to you I'm not as horrible as you think, I asked him who your mother was, but he isn't sure. Apparently, it could be one of several people, so I think that's a discussion you and he need to have."

"Discussion he and I need to have? You mean you're okay with your father and I speaking? What's gotten into you, Macie? Where are your talons?"

Just then a small knock sounded at the door and Patti Becker called out a timid, "Hello."

"For the love of God, what now?" Macie muttered as she stepped back towards the door and pulled it open.

Patti stood in the doorway looking like she was afraid to speak.

"How long have you been standing there?" Macie snapped.

"Just a few seconds. I wasn't eavesdropping, if that's what you mean. I swear I didn't hear a thing."

Patti was babbling and wringing her hands around a white cotton towel.

Macie leaned her weight against the door.

"Well, what do you want? We're in the middle of something, and I don't have time for you right now."

Patti looked like she wanted to crawl inside herself and disappear, but somehow found her voice.

"I was wondering if you're ready to get started. We're already behind schedule, and tonight's the night Carl, Steve, and Ben's film is being screened at the Charleston Film Festival, so we'd like to wrap by five... and it's almost three now."

And just like that, the old Macie was back.

"Patsy, why do I have to constantly remind you people that we roll when I say roll and we wrap when I say wrap? If they made the film, they already know what happens, so I don't think it would be a tragedy if they didn't get there in time to see it. I'll be out when

I'm ready and not a second sooner."

Macie closed the door in Patti's face and turned back to Hadleigh.

"Okay, you're unfired. I can't deal with these people like you can."

Hadleigh let out a little chuckle.

"Sorry, Macie, you're on your own, but I'll leave you with some advice. You might get further if you'd stop calling them 'you people' or at least try to remember their names. It's demeaning, and part of the reason why they hate you enough to spit in the dishes you taste each show."

Hadleigh turned back towards the desk, dropped the last of her belongings into the box, and grabbed her purse to leave.

Macie moved closer and blocked Hadleigh's path to the door. She reached up, took the box from Hadleigh's arms, and set it on the floor.

"Okay, you're right. I need to work on my people skills. If you agree to stay I'll agree to work on being more personable. I'll even let them leave on time, so they can get to their stupid film festival. Even though I can't figure out why anyone would choose to watch a documentary; those things are dreadful."

"Seriously, Macie, did you have a stroke or something? This new you are scarier than the old you."

Macie groaned and flung herself down on the couch.

"No, Hadleigh, I didn't have a stroke. I'm just tired of always being the bad guy. It's exhausting. I'm a bitch because the more I yell the more people scramble to do what I want. If you think I don't know what people say about me, or how they feel about me, you're wrong. I hate that I don't have any real friends or anyone I can trust. I doubt you'll believe this, but I had nothing to do with taking those recipes. I asked Liddy Lou and Q'Bita to create recipes for the show, but they refused because of their publishing contract, which I understood.

"Then, out of nowhere, Tony showed up with those copies. I

knew what they were, and I should have sent him packing, but Daddy said he'd take care of the fallout. You don't know how many times I've wanted to just be honest and give them back to Liddy Lou, but the show has been a hit, and I've dug the hole so deep I don't know how to crawl out without tanking the whole Macie Dixon Line. "I haven't had to work for much in life, but I've worked hard to design my brand, and I can't let it fail."

By the time she finished, Macie's face was streaked with tears and mascara.

Hadleigh sat down beside her and put her arm around her. "Okay, I'll stay, but from here on out we do things the right way, and that includes giving those recipes back and dealing with whatever the consequences might be."

Chapter 16

When the screening ended, Hadleigh excused herself and stepped outside to call Macie. Hadleigh'd been surprised when Macie called it a wrap at 4:30 saying she wasn't feeling well and wanted to rest. When Hadleigh had shown concern, Macie insisted she'd be fine and encouraged Hadleigh to go enjoy the festival with the rest of the crew.

But Hadleigh was worried, and now her call went right to voicemail. She tried two more times and got voicemail each time. It wasn't like Macie to not answer the phone, and Hadleigh was starting to feel guilty about leaving Macie alone at the studio when she wasn't feeling well.

The drive back to Castle Creek took half an hour, and still Macie wasn't answering. As Hadleigh pulled into the parking lot, she noticed Macie's bubble gum pink Hummer was still parked in its usual spot near the door.

Hadleigh parked next to Macie's SUV and climbed the few stairs to the front door. She was about to swipe her access badge when she noticed the front doors were open a crack. The TV station doors were normally locked after 5:30 PM and only accessible via access badge. Hadleigh made a mental note to mention the open doors to the station manager the next day. She and Macie often worked after hours, and while Castle Creek was usually a safe place, she didn't like the idea that someone could just walk in off the street unannounced.

She pulled the door open and stepped inside. It was unsettlingly dark, and she fumbled for the light switch on the wall, expecting to find that they'd been switched off. She was surprised to find them in the 'on' position.

Hadleigh reached for her cell phone and activated the flashlight app. She directed it at the floor a few feet in front of her and started towards Macie's dressing room.

As she made her way down the hall she heard the distant sound of the *Country Cooking With Macie* theme song. She shook her head; only Macie would be so self-absorbed that she used the theme song to her own show as a ringtone. The song played through again and then ended, having gone to voicemail.

A few feet from Macie's door, Hadleigh came to a stop. The door was open, and she could see a dark mass lying across the threshold. She inched closer, holding her breath, and almost fainted when the flashlight beam illuminated a hand and a tangle of long, blond hair.

"Oh God, Macie."

Hadleigh knelt and leaned in closer. Macie wasn't moving and didn't respond. Hadleigh reached out and gently touched Macie's hand.

"Macie, can you hear me?"

Still no reply. She reached for Macie's shoulder and gave her a gentle shake.

"Macie, wake up."

But Macie's skin was icy cold.

Hadleigh scrambled back against the wall and dialed 911.

"Dispatch. What's your emergency?"

Hadleigh's mind went temporarily blank.

"Hello, is anyone there?"

Hadleigh felt her voice cracked as she spoke.

"I, I... um... I need an ambulance, please."

A calm voice said, "What's the nature of your emergency?"

"I'm not sure," Hadleigh said. "I think my boss may have had an accident."

The rest of the conversation went by in a blur, and Hadleigh was still huddled against the wall when she heard sirens outside. She got to her feet and started towards the door when she heard Macie's cell phone ring again. The sound of the ringtone made her stomach churn as she realized somewhere someone was trying to reach Macie and they had no idea they'd never speak to her again.

Chapter 17

Orvis Burr pulled two succulent T-bone steaks off the grill just as Andy's phone rang.

"Okay, we'll be right there."

Andy ended his call and shot Orvis a look that conveyed their steak dinner was going to have to wait.

"We've got a body at the television studio. Looks like they need us both."

Orvis poured his beer over the coals and walked the plate of sizzling red meat into the kitchen as he muttered, "I'll grab my stuff and be right with you, Andy."

Orvis Burr had been the Castle Creek coroner for thirty years, and this wasn't the first meal he'd missed because of work, and probably wouldn't be the last.

A small crowd was starting to gather in the parking lot of the television studio as Andy and Orvis arrived. Deputy Mike Collins met Andy's SUV at the barricade and let them pass. Andy parked just inside the makeshift, sawhorse parameter.

As they exited Andy's SUV, Castle Creek's resident gossip columnist Spenser Penn charged the barricade with a photographer in tow.

"Sheriff Hansen, what's happening in there?" Spenser yelled.

The repeated flash from the photographer's camera temporarily blinded Andy as he turned towards the growing crowd and mustered up his authoritative voice.

"You people need to go on back home. All information will be released through our Press Office when the time is right."

He turned and started to walk away when he heard a commotion behind him. He turned back around to see Spenser Penn ducking under the barricade as his photographer wrestled with Deputy Collins. Spenser bolted toward Andy and Orvis.

"Sheriff, need I remind you that the election is only a few months away, and I'd hate for my readers to get the impression that you don't think it's necessary to share information with the press."

Andy took two quick steps towards Spenser and was about to rip into him when he felt Orvis grasp his arm.

Spenser seized the moment like a snake in an unguarded hen house.

"Hello, Orvis. Would you care to comment as to why your presence is necessary? One hardly expects to see the coroner arrive with the sheriff at a crime scene unless there's a dead body or two to be dealt with."

Orvis let go of Andy's arm and took a step towards Spenser Penn.

"Spenser, I have a quote for you." Spenser was practically salivating as he leaned closer to Orvis.

"Make sure you get this right. I'd hate to be misquoted," Orvis said.

Spenser looked about to burst with excitement.

"Castle Creek Gazette gossip hack Spenser Penn was finally silenced today when Castle Creek coroner Orvis Burr shot him in the balls with a Taser."

Andy reached for the Taser at his side and started to pull it from its harness as Spenser Penn sneered at Orvis.

"For a man in your position, Orvis, you really should have more professionalism."

Orvis glared at Spenser and held his hand out towards Andy. "Give me that Taser, Andy."

Andy took his hand off the Taser and shook his head.

"Okay, fellas, this was fun, but we have an issue that needs attention inside. Spenser, get back behind the barricade, and if I so much as hear that you or any of your staff has inched a toe over on this side, or given anyone any further grief, I will not hesitate to haul you down to my office and lock you up for impeding this investigation."

Spenser didn't know when to quit.

"So you admit this is an investigation?"

Andy reached for the Taser again and, looking directly at Spenser, said, "Here you go, Orvis. Have some fun."

Spenser Penn backed up quickly but still pressed his luck as he ducked back under the barricade.

"The two of you may think you're cute but we'll see how cute the people of Castle Creek think you are when I expose your childishness in print."

The photographer was now back on the civilian side of the barrier and Mike Collins seemed to have things under control. Andy nodded at his deputy and said loudly, "Mike, if Spenser slithers back over on this side, you have my permission to shoot him."

Deputy Collins smiled.

"With pleasure, Sheriff."

As Orvis and Andy made their way towards the front doors of the studio, Orvis glanced sideways at Andy.

"I guess we probably shouldn't rattle his cage too much before the election. You'd think anyone with half a lick of sense wouldn't vote for Chance Holleran, but people do seem to love every nasty bit of dirt Spenser calls news."

Andy bobbed his head in agreement.

"Yeah, I'd like to think I have a lock on reelection but there's a lot of people in this town who still feel I had no business running against Rex Holleran. I worry those people might have enough sway for Chance to win."

Orvis shook his head.

"Chance Holleran is a decent deputy but he's too much like his uncle Rex, if you ask me. He still has a lot to learn about right and wrong before he can climb over you and warm your chair with his ass."

Andy laughed and clapped Orvis on the back.

"Thanks for the vote of confidence, Orvis. Any chance I can talk you into being my campaign manager?"

They stepped inside and were enveloped in darkness.

"Why the hell is everyone working in the dark?"

Chance Holleran's voice replied from a few feet away as a flashlight beam cut through the darkness.

"Power's out. Looks like someone cut the main line coming into the building from outside."

"So what else have we got?" Andy asked his deputy.

"Honestly, Andy, what we've got is a huge barrel of shit. Macie Dixon is dead, and it doesn't appear to be an accident from what I've seen so far. I locked down the main scene and told everyone to stay put and not touch anything until you two got here."

"Macie Dixon? Dear God, she's just a baby. Has the family been notified yet?" Orvis asked.

"Hell no. I'm not sheriff yet. I do not want to be the one to tell Red Dixon his daughter's dead. That unpleasant task is all Andy's."

Before Andy could comment, the lights snapped on with a whoosh and he could see Macie Dixon's body lying on the floor a few feet down the hall.

"Burl Smith's on the ambulance crew tonight. His dad is the maintenance guy for the studio. Once EMS determined Macie was gone, I had Burl call his dad in to switch on the secondary power. I figured it would be better for the scene to have people working in the light so they aren't disturbing potential evidence."

"Good call," Andy said. "Get hold of Billy Jarvis and get him down here to help Mike with crowd control. It's getting kind of rowdy out there, and I need you in here. Don't tell him about Macie, though. Just tell him it's crowd control. I don't want any information getting out until I've had a chance to notify the family."

Chapter 18

Andy had just finished his examination of television station grounds and was about to go over Hadleigh's statement with Chance when his radio squelched, and a panicked Mike Collins informed him that Red and Cookie Dixon had pushed past him and were on their way inside.

"Shit! That's all I need right now. We're not even finished processing the damn scene yet."

Chance laughed.

"I bet Red's going to rip you a new one for not calling him sooner. Remind me to find out who did tell him, so I can thank them in my acceptance speech when I become sheriff."

Andy scowled at his deputy.

"You don't get to make an acceptance speech, you jackass."

Before he could say anything else, Andy heard Red Dixon's voice carrying all the way down the hall.

"Where the hell is Sheriff Hansen?"

Andy carefully stepped past the white sheet covering Macie's body and quickly moved down the hall in hopes of stopping the Dixons before they saw the body. No one, not even an ass like Red Dixon, should have to see their child like that, Andy thought to himself.

Andy rounded the corner and almost collided with Red, who looked like he was possessed. Red shoved a finger into Andy's shoulder so hard Andy felt like it went right through his skin.

"Where is my daughter? I want to see her right now."

Andy raised both hands to calm Red down but Red surprised him by grabbing both his wrists and slamming him against the wall.

"Take me to my daughter now!"

Spittle flew from Red's mouth like the foamy bark of a rabid dog.

A perfectly manicured hand ending in blood red nails appeared in Andy's face and then pressed itself into Red's chest. Cookie Dixon had a high-pitched voice that grated on your nerves like someone snapping their gum in church. "Damn it, Red, you need to calm down. We don't even know that it's Macie that's dead."

Cookie's words seemed to break something in Red. He let go of Andy, leaned back against the opposite wall, and started to sob.

"I just want to see my princess. Please tell me it isn't her."

Andy had never been a fan of Red Dixon but right now his heart was breaking for the man. He hated this part of his job, but it had to be done. He smoothed his shirt and tucked it back in then ran a hand across his face.

Andy stooped down and locked eyes with Red. Red looked up at him with tear-soaked cheeks, his face both hopeful and contorted with fear.

Andy cleared his throat and said softly, "I'm so sorry, Red."

Red Dixon made a noise that was part wail and part roar. "Nooooo. Not my baby, not my Macie."

He began sobbing again and muttering unintelligibly.

Andy looked up at Cookie who, to his surprise, looked bored.

"I know this must be a shock. I'll give the two of you a few minutes to process all this. When you're ready, I'll be out front in the lobby and I can fill you in on what we know so far."

"What you know so far? What do you mean, what you know so far? What you'd better know is where Liddy Lou Cormier is and when she is going to be arrested for killing Macie."

Cookie's words took Andy a second to process.

"Okay, slow down a minute. What does Liddy Lou Cormier have to do with any of this, and why are you assuming Macie's death was murder? We haven't established anything yet."

Cookie looked at Andy like he was the dumbest man on the planet.

"Of course it was murder, Sheriff. Macie was a young, healthy female so her death certainly wasn't natural, and the only person in this town with a reason to want Macie dead is Liddy Lou Cormier."

Andy took a deep breath and let it out slowly.

"I'm aware of the bad feelings between Macie and Miss Liddy Lou but it's way too early to jump to the conclusion that Macie was murdered or that Liddy Lou Cormier killed her. There are no outwardly visible signs of trauma or any immediately identifiable cause of death, but I promise you we will get to the bottom of this as soon as possible."

"Will you, Sheriff?" Cookie asked. "Maybe you're just dragging your heels because you're sleeping with Liddy Lou Cormier's granddaughter and arresting Liddy Lou would cause you a whole passel of problems in your love life."

Red was now standing up.

"Stop it, Cookie, just stop. My baby is dead. I don't want to argue, I just want to see my Macie."

Andy placed a hand on Red's shoulder.

"Red, you have my word. As soon as Orvis is finished I'll make arrangements for you to see Macie."

Red stifled back a sob.

"Be honest with me, Andy, did she suffer?"

"It doesn't appear that way."

Cookie snorted.

"Oh yes, I'm sure Liddy Lou Cormier weighed all her options and then chose to kill Macie with kindness."

Andy was losing his patience with Cookie Dixon, but he reminded himself the Dixons had just lost a child and he needed to cut them some slack.

"Cookie, I promise you we're going to look into every lead regardless of where it takes us."

Cookie rolled her eyes and was about to say something else when Red held up a hand and just said, "Stop, please."

Andy seized the opportunity to walk Red and Cookie to the

lobby and asked Deputy Collins to keep anyone else out of the building unless they were with law enforcement or EMS. As he made his way back towards the crime scene, he saw Cookie was making a halfhearted attempt to comfort Red. It struck Andy as odd that she seemed more annoyed than distraught.

Chapter 19

Orvis was writing up his report when Andy returned. He looked up from his tablet. "How's Red?"

"He's a mess, but I would be, too, if this was my child. I promised him we'd let him see Macie before you take her. Hope that isn't going to be too much of an issue."

Orvis nodded.

"I need an official ID, so I can let him view the body."

"What is your best guess as to COD at this point?" Andy asked.

"Well, I don't think you're going to like this much but based on what I've seen so far I'd say she was poisoned. I won't know for sure until I do the autopsy and we get some tox results back."

"Poison? Could it have been accidental?"

Orvis shook his head.

"I doubt it but I'm not ruling anything out for now. Chance found something inside I think you should see."

Andy carefully stepped around the sheet-covered body still lying in the doorway. Chance Holleran was photographing the room. He looked up as Andy entered.

"You look pretty intact. Guess old Red must have gone easy on you."

"For God's sake, Chance, the man just found out his only child is gone. I'd have let him deck me if it would have helped. He's completely devastated, and broken people can't always control themselves. Dealing with this kind of thing comes with the job, so you'd better right yourself with it if you want my badge or you sure won't be able to keep hold of it for long. Now quit your yapping and tell me what you found."

Chance crossed the room to a small table in the corner where a gift basket was sitting. The basket was full of cookies, homemade jam, and a plate of plump, gooey cinnamon buns. A bun with several bites missing was bagged separately and tagged as evidence, as was a note card Andy assumed had come with the basket.

His chest started to tighten when he saw the bright red ribbon with gold embossed lettering lying next to the basket. He'd seen Q'Bita making up similar baskets for the guest rooms at the Red Herring Inn.

Andy tugged on a pair of gloves, picked up the ribbon, and started to pull it through his fingers. The tightness in his chest quickly became a stabbing pain as the words Welcome and Red Herring Inn unwound before his eyes.

Behind him Chance cleared his throat.

"Um, you might want to look at that note."

Andy placed the ribbon back on the table next to the basket and picked up the evidence bag containing the note. He gently removed the note from the bag and saw the gold embossed RHI on the front of the card. Dread coursed through his veins as he read the note.

"Macie, I hope you'll accept this small token of peace. I feel just terrible about how I've behaved recently and want to apologize. I hope we can put the events of the last few months behind us and move on. I know cinnamon buns are your favorite, so I made these especially for you. Hope you enjoy them. Sincerely, Liddy Lou Cormier."

Andy's hand was trembling as he finished reading the note, and he could feel Chance's eyes on the back of his neck watching for a reaction. He took a deep breath and carefully placed the note back in the evidence bag and sealed it. He turned to face his deputy hoping his face didn't show the thousand emotions bubbling up inside him. "Got anything else you want to show me?"

"What else do you need? Macie obviously opened the basket, started to eat one of those cinnamon buns, and died from some type of poison before she could even finish it. The part that gets me is why Liddy Lou Cormier would be so dumb as to use a gift basket from her own inn and then further implicate herself by including a signed note."

Andy's first reaction was to defend Liddy Lou but given the circumstances he wasn't sure what to think.

"I just cannot believe Liddy Lou Cormier has it in her to commit murder. The whole thing seems too staged to me. I understand Macie's assistant found the body. What does she have to say about all this?"

Chance pulled out a notebook and flipped through the pages. "Well, Miss Banks says they wrapped early today so the crew could attend the film festival in Charleston. Macie wasn't feeling well and decided to stay here. I asked her about the gift basket and she stated it wasn't here when she left so it must have arrived sometime after 4:45 PM.

She tried calling Macie on her way back from Charleston and became concerned when Macie wasn't picking up so decided to come here to check on her.

Probably the most useful thing she gave us was that the front doors are locked after 5:30 PM and only accessible by pass key. When she got here the doors were open a crack and the power was already out."

"That's it?" Andy asked.

"Yep. Not much useful there."

"Well, maybe, maybe not. Track down the station manager or security folks and see if they have cameras or door access reports that might tell us who was coming and going today."

"How come I'm doing grunt work? Thought that's why we had Mike."

Andy could feel the back of his neck starting to get warm, and his jaw was twitching. It took all his self-control sometimes to not lose his temper with Chance.

"Because Mike is busy dealing with crowd control. If you want, I can switch you two out, and you can stand outside in front of half the town with your thumb up your ass. I hear Spenser Penn is out there; might make for a few good promo pictures for your campaign."

Chance rolled his eyes at Andy and flipped him the bird on the way out the door.

Orvis Burr popped his head in the doorway and let Andy know they were going to move the body to a gurney in the hallway so the Dixons could have a few minutes before EMS left for the morgue.

"Okay. Once you're done I'm going to close this door. There's a few things Chance documented that I want to look over before we seal up the scene."

"Anything telling?" asked Orvis.

Andy sighed, thinking back to the conversation he'd had with Q'Bita about Liddy Lou being close to exploding.

"Yeah, plenty. I'm just not convinced they're telling me what they appear to be, or at least I hope they aren't."

Chapter 20

They had all gathered in the Library. The scent of freshly brewed coffee and lilacs perfumed the room. Liddy Lou folded the morning paper and sat it on the table. Macie Dixon's death was splashed all over the front page of the Castle Creek Gazette. Her shoulders slumped as she heaved a loud sigh and glanced about at her family.

"Well, this certainly wasn't how I expected my morning to start."

"I'm sorry to spring this on you first thing in the morning. Andy called late last night with the news, but I didn't want to wake you," Q'Bita said as she refilled her grandmother's coffee cup.

As she topped off her brother's cup, Beecher asked, "Did he give any indication about what happened?"

Before Q'Bita could answer, Rene chimed in, "Am I the only one who thinks it's absurd and unconscionable that Spenser Penn can make it sound like Liddy Lou is a suspect? God forbid he'd wait to see what really happened and report the facts, but no, spitting venom sells more papers."

Q'Bita finished topping off everyone's coffee and waited for her brother-in-law's tirade to end.

"Andy couldn't say much because it's an active investigation, but he felt that based on recent events some people might speculate Nana was somehow responsible for Macie's death."

Beecher placed his hand on his grandmother's shoulder and gave it a gentle squeeze.

"Nana, I don't want you worrying yourself about any of this. We all know you had nothing to do with this, and I'm sure Sheriff Hansen and his people will have this all cleared up by the end of the day."

"And what happens if he doesn't?" asked Rene. "Are we just going to sit back and let Spenser Penn tarnish Liddy Lou's good name like some hand-me-down silver-plated serving tray? I say we make Kent Haskell earn his retainer for once and have him sue the dockers off that hack for slander and defamation of character."

"Actually, we have an appointment with Kent at 11:45 this morning. I'm sure he'll get this all worked out as soon as possible," said Kari.

The second Kari finished speaking, both Beecher and Rene started up again, one talking over the other, each explaining what they thought should be done next.

Liddy Lou clanked her spoon against the side of her coffee cup, and it made a horrible noise. She sat up straighter in her chair and cleared her throat.

"First, I want to say that I love and appreciate that each of you is willing to do whatever you think is best to protect me; however, I'd like to point out I am still perfectly capable of taking care of myself, so stop treating me like I'm some fragile little bird. I did not kill anyone... yet!" Liddy Lou rose from her chair, placed her cup and saucer on the table in front of her, and left the room without a look back.

An awkward silence hung in the air. They all knew their matriarch could be feisty at times, but she seldom directed it their way. Jamie was the one to finally say what they'd all been thinking.

"Okay, then. I get the feeling Liddy Lou was kind of upset with us but please tell me that none of us is planning on letting her try to handle this on her own."

As if they shared a single mind, the entire Block family blurted out a collective, "No."

Chapter 21

The rest of the day was like walking on egg shells, with everyone on edge about Macie Dixon's murder. Q'Bita was exhausted. She tumbled into bed just before midnight and was in the middle of a pleasant dream involving warm, buttery croissants and thick, French drinking chocolate when the sound of a ringing phone pulled her back to the real world. She plucked her cell phone from the nightstand and saw Jamie's name.

"Q'B-doll, you awake? You're never going to believe what I dug up."

Q'Bita felt her stomach do a little flip.

"Jamie, please tell me digging didn't involve accessing databases you have no business being in."

"Girl, please, I'm a professional. They'll never even know I was there. Besides, this is good stuff, and it just might keep Liddy Lou out of jail."

"Damn it, Jamie. It won't do any good to clear Nana if you end up in jail instead. You know you'll do serious time if you get caught again."

"Q'Bita, I love you, but can we just hit the pause button on the lecture and talk about what I found?"

"Okay, but you have to promise, no more—"

"Sure. Fine. I promise. Now stop talking and just listen. It seems Macie Dixon should have checked her references a little more closely. Her food stylist, Patti Becker, has been arrested twice for assault and once for violating the terms of a PFA order. Sounds like someone has a few anger issues."

"Okay, but what motive would she have to kill Macie? Besides, Andy didn't mention any signs of a struggle."

"I don't solve crimes, I gather information, Q'Bita, and I have more to share as soon as you stop interrupting me."

"There's more?" Q'Bita could hear Jamie clicking his teeth in frustration. "Okay, sorry, go on."

"Turns outs Patti isn't the only one with something to hide. Hadleigh Banks has a sealed juvenile record. Fortunately, I have mad skills and was able to crack that seal like a walnut. She may seem all shy and polite on the surface, but she apparently has enough balls to have racked up several charges related to breaking and entering and records theft."

Q'Bita was wide awake now and her mind was spinning.

"So Hadleigh is a thief? Do you think Macie knew this? Maybe she's the one who stole Nana's recipes for Macie."

"I guess it's possible," Jamie said. "From what I could piece together, she got nailed for B&E twice. One was a girls' group home, and the other was a Sisters of Catholic Mercy Convent. The judge showed her leniency because the records she stole were her own. She's adopted and was trying to find out about her birth parents. She got probation, community service, and court ordered counseling but we both know that doesn't mean she'd never cross the line again. I know I sure have."

Q'Bita was quiet for a few seconds as it dawned on her how similar Hadleigh's early life seemed to Jamie's. He'd veered off track, too, until Liddy Lou took him in.

Q'Bita knew any further lecture would be wasted words so she dropped it.

"Wow. Sounds like she had a rough start in life."

Jamie chuckled but Q'Bita could hear the sadness behind it. "Yeah, sounds like she and I might have more than a few things in common. No wonder I think she's hot."

This time it was Q'Bita who laughed.

"I still want to choke you for taking such a risk, but you did good. Let's keep this between us for now until I can figure out how to spoon-feed the information to Andy without having to tell him where I got it."

Jamie agreed, and they made plans to get together in the morning, before Jamie's shift to brainstorm what to do next. Q'Bita tried to fall back asleep but her mind was racing, trying to process everything Jamie had shared, and what if anything it might have to do with Macie Dixon's death.

Jamie came in around 10 and they were deep into their brainstorming session when Q'Bita heard the crunch of gravel coming from the parking lot. Her breath caught in her throat when she saw that it was Andy. She turned to Jamie, a look of panic on her face.

"I have no idea why he's here. I hope it isn't more bad news."

"Breathe, Q'B-doll. Everything is going to be fine."

Jamie's body language didn't match his reassuring words.

Q'Bita greeted Andy at the door.

"Hello, handsome. This is a nice surprise."

She stretched up on her tip toes and kissed his cheek. He smelled like soap and fresh air and she wanted to lose herself in that smell.

Andy smiled and tucked a stray curl behind her ear.

"I hope you'll still be feeling that way when I leave. I have some questions for you about Macie's case, and I'm worried you'll be upset with me for asking."

All hope that her day was going to get any better drained out of Q'Bita as she stepped back to let Andy into the kitchen.

"Hey, Sheriff Hansen. How're you doing?"

"Doing fine, Jamie. How about yourself?"

"That depends. Are you here to tell us you've solved the case and Liddy Lou has nothing to worry about?"

Andy looked from Jamie to Q'Bita and blushed a little.

"I'm afraid not."

"Well, I'm not doing too good, then," Jamie said dryly.

Q'Bita grabbed a glass and poured Andy some sweet tea.

"Thanks, Q'Bita."

Andy took a few sips and seemed lost in thought as he wiped at the condensation trickling down the glass.

"So, have there been any developments in the case?"

"Yes, there have, and that's why I'm here."

Andy squirmed in his seat and took a long swig of his iced tea then looked in Jamie's direction.

"Some of these questions are kind of personal and it might be better to have a one-on-one conversation," Andy said to Q'Bita.

Jamie gave Q'Bita a wounded look. She was torn, but if it turned out that Andy's questions implicated her nana, she knew she'd want Jamie there for emotional support.

"I appreciate you wanting to be discreet but Jamie's a part of this family and anything having to do with Liddy Lou is going to be shared with him anyhow, so I'd like him to stay if that's okay."

Andy looked uncomfortable and Q'Bita hoped he wasn't upset with her.

"Okay, but anything I say here cannot be shared outside your family. That means not a word to Kent Haskell, Evie Newsome, or anyone else until it becomes public knowledge. The mayor would have my badge if he knew I was sharing this with you."

Jamie and Q'Bita both shook their heads in agreement.

"First, I want to make it clear we're still reviewing all the evidence and we haven't yet labeled anyone a suspect."

"Wait, suspect? Are you saying Macie was murdered, then?" Jamie asked, shooting Q'Bita a nervous glance.

Andy's neck was turning red and a bead of sweat trickled down the side of his face. He stuttered a little when he spoke.

"I'm, I'm afraid it's looking that way. Orvis thinks she was poisoned. He's waiting for the tox results to come back later this afternoon. We should know for sure then."

"When you first came in you said you had questions for me about Macie's death. I don't know much about poison, unless it's food poisoning, so I'm not sure I can be much help," Q'Bita said.

Andy drained the last of his iced tea.

"I'm not so concerned about the poison itself; the tox screen will tell me everything I need to know there. I'm more interested in figuring out how Macie ingested the poison."

Jamie and Q'Bita exchanged confused looks.

"I'm not following you," Q'Bita said.

Andy took a deep breath and let it out slowly.

"Q'Bita, do you still put a plate of cinnamon buns in each of your welcome baskets for your guests?"

"Yes. They're Nana's secret recipe, and they're a huge hit with our guests. You wouldn't believe how many comments we get about them in our online reviews. Right after we opened, Appalachian Travel Magazine ran an article about the Inn, and the reporter loved them so much she used a picture of them in her article. What does this have to do with Macie's death, though?"

"When we processed the scene, there was a Red Herring Inn welcome basket in the room. It contained a plate of cinnamon buns. We found one on the floor with a few bites missing. I'm guessing we're going to find that's how Macie ingested the poison."

Q'Bita's hands started to shake, and she felt dizzy.

"How can you be sure it was one of our baskets? We buy them in bulk from Sammie Hake's flower shop. Anyone in town could buy one just like it."

"The basket had one of your red bows on it, and there was a note on the table next to the basket."

"Note? What kind of note?" Jamie asked.

"It appears to be an apology note from Liddy Lou claiming the basket was a peace offering."

Q'Bita couldn't believe what Andy had just said. There was no amount of circumstantial evidence in the world that could convince her that her nana was a killer. She could feel tears stinging her eyes and was grasping for something to say when Jamie asked, "Are you going to arrest Liddy Lou?"

Andy held his hands up in surrender.

"I'm not arresting anyone yet. I'm only sharing this because I was hoping you could help me come up with a reasonable explanation for how the basket ended up being in Macie's dressing room. Something about all this doesn't feel right to me but I'm getting a butt-ton of pressure from the Dixons to make an arrest. I need to get all the facts as quickly as possible."

Their conversation was interrupted when Andy's phone rang. He excused himself and stepped outside to take the call. When Andy returned he had a troubled look.

"Everything okay?" Q'Bita asked.

Andy pocketed his phone and ran his hand through his hair. "I'm not sure. That was Chance. I sent him down to the television station to interview some of the production crew and he said one of the crew was acting kind of nervous and disappeared before he could ask her any questions. Could be nothing, but it seems kind of odd."

"I don't suppose you can tell us which crew member it was, could you?" Jamie asked.

Q'Bita shot Jamie a distressed look and mouthed for him to be quiet hoping Andy wouldn't notice, but he did.

"Um, something you two care to share with me? I sense a little tension all of the sudden."

Jamie started to say something but Q'Bita spoke over him. "No, nothing. Everything is all fine, I swear."

Q'Bita could hear the quiver in her voice.

"With all due respect, Q'Bita, you're not very good at hiding things from me," Andy said with a frown. "If there's something I should know, it's better you tell me now."

Q'Bita's heart was pounding and her ears were ringing. She truly cared for Andy, but Jamie was her best friend and she just couldn't risk getting him in trouble. She tried her best to hide the rising fear bubbling up inside her as she contemplated what to say to Andy.

"Oh, for God's sake, Q'Bita, just tell him what we know before you implode. If it can help Liddy Lou, it doesn't matter what happens to me."

"Jamie, shut up."

Q'Bita hadn't meant for the words to come out so harsh and regretted them as soon as they were out.

The look of hurt and shock on Jamie's face hit Q'Bita like a gut punch, and she felt like crying.

Jamie crossed to her side of the counter and softly punched her shoulder.

"Q'B-doll, it's alright. I know you want to protect me, but I knew the risk when I took it. We have to tell Andy."

It suddenly dawned on Andy why Q'Bita seemed so upset. Like Jamie, Andy was a Castle Creek native and was aware of Jamie's past troubles with the Feds.

"If this has to do with Jamie violating his probation, I can probably look the other way provided you keep my name out of this if he manages to get himself caught again."

Q'Bita looked up at Andy in disbelief.

"You know about Jamie's probation?"

"Of course. I have to keep track of all felony violators in Castle Creek while they're still on parole. Especially the ones with federal violations. It's part of my job."

Andy's face had softened a bit, and Q'Bita could feel herself relax a little as Jamie shared what he'd uncovered with Andy.

"Wow, that was some serious detective work, and it certainly raises some questions I'll need to look into further, but it still doesn't explain how the Red Herring Inn welcome basket or the note from Liddy Lou ended up in Macie's room."

Q'Bita chewed on her bottom lip as she tried to come up with an explanation, but she had nothing. She paced back and forth as she filled their glasses with iced tea and set out a pear and chai cream tart she'd been recipe-testing for an upcoming class.

"Can't you just dust the note for prints or analyze the handwriting?" Jamie asked.

"We already checked and found no prints, and the note was typed and printed out. My guys are still working on determining the type of printer."

Q'Bita cut into the pie and plated three servings. As she placed one in front of Andy they made eye contact. His look was warm and comforting but she couldn't help wondering if someday soon she'd look at him and only be able to see the man who arrested her nana for a murder she didn't commit.

Chapter 22

For the second time that week Andy's love of pie had to take a back seat to work. Three bites in, Mike Collins called to say he and Chance had intercepted Patti Becker in the process of leaving town and they'd parked her in an interrogation room for him to question her.

Andy was still steaming as he drove to the station. When he'd asked Mike why they didn't just question Patti themselves, Mike had hesitated, then admitted Chance thought the case was a career death sentence and that he and Mike should distance themselves from it as much as possible. Andy wasn't sure if he was angrier at his deputies for being idiots or because they were right about the case being a career killer.

He tried to think about something less upsetting as he glanced over at Q'Bita. She gave him a smile that made him melt. This was also the second time this week he'd let her tag along to the station. This, too, was probably a career killer, but he couldn't help himself. When it came to Q'Bita Block he was powerless to tell her no.

"Thanks again for agreeing to let me come with you, Andy. Hopefully, whatever is going on with Patti Becker will clear my nana, so we can put this mess behind us and get back to normal."

"Well, I hope so, too, Q'Bita, but let's not get ahead of ourselves. Just because Patti has a record doesn't make her a killer. As much as I want to clear Liddy Lou—and believe me, I do—I need to be extra careful with this case. The Dixons are already squawking at me about why I haven't arrested your nana. Cookie Dixon came right out and accused me of stalling because of our relationship. Red's also been hinting that he's going to back Chance in the election. It wouldn't surprise me if Chance has been feeding the

Dixons information about this investigation, so you gotta lay low again when we get to the station."

One of the perks of being sheriff was having an office with its own private entrance from the back-parking lot. Andy opened the door and took a quick glance around his office to make sure it was empty. He motioned for Q'Bita to come in, then moved to the door that opened to the bull pen and locked it.

Andy moved closer and bent down to give her a kiss as he pulled her into a hug. He held her close for a minute and then said, "I'd better head out there. Stay in here, out of sight, and I'll be back as soon as I can."

Q'Bita was afraid if she let go this might be the last hug they shared. She felt bad he was under so much pressure to solve Macie Dixon's murder, but she also knew her nana was innocent.

If Q'Bita was wrong, and Patti wasn't responsible, Andy might have no choice but to arrest her nana. She wasn't sure she could forgive him for that.

The next hour crept by at a snail's pace. Q'Bita passed the time by making a list of all the questions she thought Andy should be asking about the case before making an arrest. When the phone on Andy's desk rang, it scared her so badly she almost peed herself. One look at the phone's LED screen told her it was from Castle Creek Coroner Orvis Burr.

Picking up the phone would be a huge violation of Andy's trust, but she needed to know if the tox results were back and if Orvis had determined the cause of death. The information might be key to proving her nana's innocence.

She'd just finished asking Orvis what he'd discovered when Andy opened the door. He gave her a questioning look as he entered the office, and Q'Bita lost her nerve.

"Um, hold on a second. Andy's just walked in, so maybe you should tell him." Q'Bita handed him the receiver. "It's Orvis."

Andy took the phone and shot her a raised eyebrow.

"Hey, Orvis. What's up?"

Q'Bita could only hear one side of the conversation, and it was maddening.

"Let me guess, COD was acute toxicity due to cyanide poisoning."

Andy paused to let Orvis answer.

"Wait, are you sure? That can't be right. We just got a confession ten minutes ago. Macie's food stylist admitted to putting ground bitter almonds in food and wine Macie consumed a few hours before her death, so strychnine doesn't make any sense."

At the mention of strychnine, all the air sucked out of Q'Bita's chest and she made a small gasping noise.

"You absolutely sure the cyanide levels were too low to be COD?"

Andy was quiet as he finished listening to what Orvis had to say.

"Oh, damn it to hell."

Andy kicked the corner of his desk with the toe of his boot. His outburst caused Q'Bita to jump a little in her seat.

"Thanks for the additional info, Orvis. I'll make some inquiries, then."

Andy hung up and gave Q'Bita a pained, serious look.

"So I'm guessing you heard, the COD was strychnine poisoning."

Q'Bita couldn't find her voice so she nodded in reply.

"And I'm sure you also heard me telling Orvis that Patti Becker has confessed. Problem is, Patti's version of events doesn't match up with the COD. Orvis also told me this is the second case of strychnine poisoning in Castle Creek this week."

"That was an accident. Nana had nothing to do with it."

"Q'Bita, you need to tell me what happened with Rolfie."

Deep down, Q'Bita knew that Andy was just doing his job, but she didn't like what he was implying.

"That depends. Are you asking as a boyfriend or as the sheriff?" Her tone was a little harsher then she'd intended.

A look of hurt briefly flickered across Andy's face.

"Wow, would my answer really make a difference in what you tell me?"

"Like I said, what happened to Rolfie was an accident. He got into gopher bait in the barn. If Patti Becker has confessed, I don't understand why you're not satisfied with that."

Andy sat down in the chair opposite Q'Bita.

"Trust me, sweetheart, I don't believe your nana killed Macie Dixon, but my job requires me to follow the evidence, and right now there seems to be an overwhelming pile of it pointing at Liddy Lou.

"Ms. Becker claims she only used a small amount of the ground bitter almonds, just enough to make Macie sick. That seems to coincide with what Orvis found. The cyanide levels weren't even large enough to be considered a contributing factor."

"Does this mean you're going to arrest my nana, then?"

Andy sighed and slouched down in his chair.

"No but I am going to have to bring her in for questioning."

Q'Bita stood, picked up her purse, and started towards the door to the parking lot. A million emotions were fighting for space in her mind, and she knew if she said another word it would probably be something she'd regret later.

"Now, Q'Bita, don't get yourself all worked up. Give me a few minutes to wrap things up here and I'll take you back home."

"No, that's okay. You do what you need to do, sheriff. In the meantime, at least one of us needs to focus on figuring out who the real killer is before my nana ends up taking the blame."

She didn't wait for Andy to reply before opening the door to the parking lot and letting it slam shut behind her.

Andy started after Q'Bita but stopped when his desk phone rang. He looked at the LED screen and felt his blood pressure rising. Red Dixon was the last person he wanted to deal with right now. Andy ran his fingers through his hair and let loose a string of obscenities. He couldn't believe how quickly this day had turned to shit.

Chapter 23

As she made her way down Main Street, Q'Bita was still angry and so wrapped up in her own thoughts that she walked right past Rene without noticing him.

"Um, hello. Earth to Q'Bita. What has your G-string all in a tangle, gorgeous?"

The sound of Rene's voice got her attention, and she turned to see where it was coming from. Her anger faded to amusement as she watched her brother-in-law prancing towards her. He was wearing a lemon chiffon tank top that was two sizes too small and floral-patterned Bermuda shorts in shades of coral and sea foam. They looked like he'd stolen the fabric from the couch cushions of a retirement home. He'd accessorized this hot mess with a pair of cork-heeled, wedge sandals with flowered toe thongs in bright peach, identical to the pair Q'Bita was wearing.

As if the outfit wasn't bad enough, he was carrying a baby blue, lace parasol in one hand and Rolfie in the other.

As Rene drew closer, he held up the angry-looking feline for Q'Bita to see. Rolfie was wearing a spiked collar and a vest with the word KILLER spelled out across the chest in blood-red rhinestones.

"Doesn't my baby just look precious?" Rene squealed. "I thought he deserved a spa day and some retail therapy after all he's been through. It's a wonder he doesn't need actual therapy after a near-death experience like that. What on earth was Liddy Lou thinking leaving poison laying around where Rolfie could get at it?"

As usual, Rene's voice projected like a Mr. Microphone.

"Rene, not so loud. Nana has enough people suspecting her already. The last thing we need is to have everyone in town thinking she's stockpiling poison."

Rene gave her an annoyed look.

"Lord, Q'Bita, you're starting to sound like Beecher. I know it was an accident, but I fail to understand why the rest of you don't seem to think the near-death of a beloved family member is a tragedy."

Q'Bita could feel a massive headache starting to form behind her eyes.

"Speaking of my brother, do you know where he is?"

"He's out at that horrid cabin, no doubt traipsing around the woods, letting every tick in the county infect him with Lyme's disease or Ebola or God knows what. I swear sometimes he wants me to be a widow, which would be a travesty, because my perfect porcelain skin shouldn't be concealed behind a black lace veil."

"Can you call him and get him back here for me? Something's come up regarding Macie's case, and I need to talk to him."

"Seriously? You want me to drag Beecher all the way back to town so you can chat when I'm right here? I'm not chopped liver, you know. If I were, Rolfie would have eaten me long ago."

Q'Bita's headache was now a reality but she knew it was best to humor Rene rather than dismiss him when he got like this.

"My apologies, your fabulousness. I didn't mean to imply you would not be part of the conversation."

"Well, then, that's better. Rolfie and I forgive you. Now entertain him while I call Beecher. Oh, and make sure to shield his eyes. He's been through too much already this week and I don't want to damage his retinas by overexposing him to UV rays. Besides, he doesn't have the cheek bones to pull off glasses."

Q'Bita stifled a laugh as people walking by gawked at Rene. He was a bit much for most folks in Castle Creek but that didn't matter to her. She loved his drama and his eclectic sense of fashion, but most of all, she loved how much he loved her brother.

She took a deep breath and scratched Rolfie between the ears. He nuzzled her chin, and she could feel her tension starting to drain.

"Okay, boy," she whispered to him. "You have to help me keep this drama queen focused until Beecher gets here. If we're going to keep this family together, we have a murder to solve."

Chapter 24

Andy answered the phone and instantly regretted it.

"Don't bother with pleasantries, Hansen. The only thing I want to hear from you is that you've done your job and have Liddy Lou Cormier in custody."

"Hello, Red."

Andy pulled out his chair and sat down. The weight of the last few days finally sank into his bones as Red Dixon continued to chew his ass. After several more minutes of cussing and spitting, Red finally paused to take a breath.

"Red, I assure you we're following every possible lead in this case and will solve it as fast as we can."

"Well, you sure as hell can't do that if you're wasting your time taking false confessions from disgruntled employees. You need to get your head out of your ass, get over to the Red Herring Inn, and arrest Liddy Lou Cormier. If you can't do your job, I'd be more than glad to ask my friends on the town council to relieve you and appoint a replacement who will."

Andy gritted his teeth and made a mental note to kick Chance's ass for leaking details of the case to the Dixons.

"That won't be necessary, Red. I have every intention of questioning Liddy Lou Cormier before the end of the day."

"Questioning? There's nothing to question, Hansen. I have it on very good authority my daughter's cause of death was the same exact poison that almost killed that monstrosity the Blocks call a cat. That's not a coincidence, that's a smoking gun."

Andy tried to reason with Red but Red cut him off mid-sentence.

"Now you listen to me, Hansen. If Liddy Lou Cormier isn't in custody by the end of the day, I'm gonna shove a battalion of lawyers so far up your ass you couldn't shit 'em out even if you were doing a prune juice cleanse."

Andy took a deep breath and reminded himself Red wasn't someone to take lightly even under ideal circumstances, and the last few days had been anything but ideal.

"Red, I can't even imagine what you're going through right now so I'm going to be the bigger man here and let that last bit slide, but you need to calm down and quit barking at me like I work for you, because I don't. I will continue to work this case until it's solved but I will not have you or anyone else tell me how to do my job. I will call you when we have any information worth sharing."

Andy hung up before Red could jump all over him again. He was about to get up and go rip Chance a new a-hole when he noticed the tablet on his desk. Q'Bita had apparently been making a list while she waited. Across the top in big block letters it read, *Questions Andy Should Be Asking.*

Well, that's not insulting at all, he thought to himself.

He tore the list from the pad and shoved it in his pocket. Apparently Red Dixon wasn't the only one who needed to be reminded he was still the sheriff and still in charge of this investigation.

He yanked open the door to the bull pen and spotted Chance on his cell phone. Startled, the deputy stared back at him like a cat who'd been caught with one paw in the bird cage.

"Damn it, Chance. Tell Red your ass is on the clock, and while it is, you take orders from me. I want you to get the hell off the phone and go book Patti Becker."

Chance told Red he'd call him back later and hung up.

"Why the hell am I booking Patti Becker? We already know she didn't kill Macie."

Andy stepped into the bull pen, slamming his office door behind him. Chance and Mike were looking at him like he might burst into flames at any second.

"Okay, I've had enough shit to last me a life time today, so both of you need to cut the crap and start acting like you're cops, not halfwits. I understand Patti Becker isn't our killer, but she still admitted to poisoning Macie. In case you two idiots need a teachable moment, that's a punishable crime."

"Jeez, Andy, you sound stressed. Maybe you should take a couple of days off and let us handle this case."

Chance's arrogant smirk agitated Andy even more than his comment, and it took every ounce of self-restraint Andy had not to pull his gun and shoot Chance in the face.

"Maybe I wouldn't be so stressed if you weren't leaking information to the Dixons every five minutes. Which, by the way, stops now. If it happens again, you're suspended until this investigation is resolved, and if you think I'm kidding, just try me."

Andy didn't wait for a reply before turning and slamming his office door behind him again.

As Andy drove down Main Street, on his way out to the Red Herring Inn, he spotted Q'Bita and Rene. He pulled over and rolled down the passenger side window.

"Q'Bita, can I have a word with you, please?"

As Q'Bita approached the open window, Andy noticed she looked a little more relaxed than when she'd stormed out of his office. She was biting her lip like she always did when she was nervous. He thought it was cute, and he momentarily forgot why he'd called her over in the first place.

"Business or pleasure?" she asked with a nervous chuckle.

Andy reached into his pocket, pulled out the crumpled list, and handed it out the window to her.

"I think you forgot something in my office. It looked important."

Q'Bita smoothed out the paper and her cheeks flushed.

"Oh my God, Andy, I'm sorry. It's not what it looks like."

"Really? 'Cause it looks to me like Red Dixon isn't the only person around here who thinks I'm not capable of solving this murder. I expected this from him, but honestly, coming from you… I gotta admit it stings, Q'Bita."

"I, I don't know what to say. I never meant to imply you weren't doing your job. I was only trying to help by doing some digging on my own."

"Q'Bita, we've been through this already. I need you to stay out of this and let me and my guys do our job. If your nana is innocent, then she doesn't have anything to worry about. I'll get to the bottom of this."

"If she's innocent?" Andy could hear the hurt in Q'Bita's voice. "So you do think she's a suspect, then."

Andy didn't want to hurt Q'Bita, but he knew he had to be honest with her about needing to question Liddy Lou.

"I don't want to think that, sweetheart, but the evidence is piling up, and right now a lot of it is pointing at your nana. I'm headed to your place now to ask her a few questions if you want to come along."

"I appreciate the offer, but I'm going to pass. I'm going to go see Kent Haskell, and I'll have him give me a ride home. I think it's best if he's there sooner rather than later."

"Okay, then. I'll see you when you get there, I guess."

Andy's voice rose at the end like he was asking her a question but Q'Bita had nothing more to say so she turned back to Rene until Andy drove away.

Chapter 25

A few miles outside of town Andy's phone rang again. Deep down he hoped it was Q'Bita calling to say she wasn't as upset with him as it had seemed a few minutes ago, but with the day he was having it was more likely Red Dixon calling for round two.

Andy pulled out his phone and was glad to see it was just Mike Collins.

"Hey, Mike. What's up?"

"On a scale of one to ten, how calm are you right now, boss?"

"Honestly, Mike, I'm about a seventeen in the wrong direction, but I have a feeling it's only going to get worse as the day goes on."

"I guess you won't be surprised then that I got some bad news for ya."

"Oh, joy," Andy said as he pulled over to the side of the road. "Go ahead. Let's hear it."

"You stormed out so fast I didn't get a chance to tell you the Lab guys called. They were able to lift one set of prints off the note card, and they belonged to Macie Dixon."

"Damn it. Not the news I was hoping for," Andy said.

"Sorry to say it only gets worse from here. We finally got the security camera footage from the TV studio, and it clearly shows Liddy Lou Cormier entering the front door just before the cameras go down."

"What? You have to be shitting me. You mean to tell me Liddy Lou Cormier just waltzed in the front door with a basket full of poison cinnamon buns and didn't even try to hide it from the cameras?"

"Well, not exactly. When the cameras picked her up she didn't have the basket. Chance figures she must have had the basket delivered earlier in the day and then stopped by to make sure Macie had taken the bait."

"It's possible, I guess, but it still doesn't add up. Liddy Lou Cormier is not a stupid woman, and I can't believe she'd set out to kill Macie Dixon and make it so obvious."

"Well, you know what they say, boss. The best place to hide something is in plain sight. Could be she planned this whole thing to look like a set-up hoping we'd waste time trying to find a killer that didn't exist."

"Christ, Mike, you've been spending too much time with Chance. I said she wasn't stupid, I didn't say she was a criminal mastermind. Is it safe to assume Chance has already shared this info with Red?"

Mike hesitated but eventually confirmed what Andy already suspected.

"Well, that's just frickin' fantastic. The next person who releases details to anyone not employed by this department is going to be picking up trash and directing traffic permanently. Make sure you pass that along to Chance when you get off the phone. Have him call me if he needs help comprehending any of the big words."

Andy could hear Mike nervously drumming his fingers on the desk and knew he'd made his point to at least one of his deputies.

"I'm headed out to the Red Herring Inn now to question Liddy Lou, so we'll see what she has to say about all this."

"There's one more thing. The Lab guys narrowed down the printer used for the note card. It's an Epson Expression Premium XP-640 Small-in-One All-in-One. I did some digging and found out Herschel Vance carries them in The Paper Box and only sold three since he started carrying them. All three were sold to Tom Block a few months ago."

Andy groaned. This mess just kept getting worse.

Andy arrived at the Red Herring Inn and found Tom and Beecher Block waiting for him on the front porch. They waived as he pulled up, and it seemed genuinely friendly, which eased his tension a little, but not completely. He hated being here. He knew what a strain it was putting on his relationship with Q'Bita and, to a lesser extent, her family. There was no way he could see Liddy Lou Cormier as a killer, but he had a duty to follow the evidence even if it put him at odds with those he cared for. He just hoped Liddy Lou could provide a plausible explanation for all this before Red Dixon forced his hand and he had to take her in.

"Afternoon, Andy," Tom called from the porch as Andy approached the steps.

"Tom. Beecher. How're you fellas doing this afternoon?"

Beecher remained quiet, but Tom let out a half-hearted laugh.

"We've had better days, but then again I'm guessing you have, too."

Andy nodded in agreement as he reached the top of the steps and shook their hands.

"I'm guessing Q'Bita or Rene already gave you a heads-up that I was coming."

This time it was Beecher who laughed.

"Q'Bita told us to expect you. Rene was too busy trying to Google the number for the National Guard to let them know we're under attack. He acted like you were coming with a full SWAT team and planning to burn Nana at the stake."

"Wow. I promise it's nothing so extreme. Some things have come up, and I can't put off asking Liddy Lou about them any longer. I hope you know I don't want to be here, and I wouldn't if there was any other way."

Tom patted Andy on the back and steered him towards the front door.

"Of course, Andy. You're just doing your job. Liddy Lou is innocent so there's no reason for any of us to get all worked up. You and your guys will find the real killer, and this will all blow over in a few days."

As he entered the Red Herring Inn, Andy wished he shared Tom's confidence.

Tom led Andy to the library while Beecher went to fetch Liddy Lou. A few minutes later Andy heard the bell over the front door chime.

"If you'll excuse me for a minute, Andy, that's probably Kent. I'll let him know we're in here."

At the mention of Kent Haskell's name Andy felt his blood pressure start to climb. Kent was the only defense attorney in Castle Creek, and damn good at his job. He was a nice enough guy, but his job often put him and Andy at odds. Any hope of having a casual conversation with Liddy Lou had now vanished.

As Tom and Kent entered the library, Andy saw Q'Bita walk past the door. She looked angry and didn't even bother to acknowledge him. He hadn't much time to dwell on it before Beecher and Liddy Lou arrived.

Liddy Lou gave Kent a double cheek air kiss and thanked him for coming on such short notice, then turned to Andy. "Sheriff, I hope you don't mind I asked Kent to join us."

Andy stood and waited for Liddy Lou to take her seat opposite him and next to Kent.

"I don't mind at all. Kent, always nice to see you."

Andy nodded in Kent's direction and noticed Kent's barely concealed look of doubt.

Kent was the first so speak.

"Sheriff, would you mind greatly if I had a few minutes with Liddy Lou and Tom before we start? As I'm sure you're aware, Ms. Cormier has no criminal record so has little experience in dealing with an interrogation. I think it's only fair that I make sure she's aware of all her rights and has been given the proper legal counsel before answering any of your questions."

Several replies raced through Andy's mind at once, none of which were polite or professional, but he reminded himself Kent was just doing his job. He also reminded himself he didn't want to do anything to further upset Q'Bita.

"No problem. I'll be out on the porch. When you're ready, just give me a holler."

Andy paced back and forth trying to decide if he should go try talking to Q'Bita before they got started. He was about to go around the back to the cooking school entrance when Tom appeared in the doorway and said they were ready for him.

As Andy entered the library, he could feel the tension in the air. He took his original seat across from Liddy Lou and Kent.

"If you're ready, Liddy Lou, I guess we can get started."

Liddy Lou nodded her head, gave Andy a forced smile, then turned to look at Kent Haskell.

"If you don't mind, Sheriff Hansen, before we begin I'd like to know if these questions are being asked because Ms. Cormier is considered a suspect or if they are just informational to your investigation."

"I'm still trying to determine that, Kent. That's why I'm here."

"Very well, then, Sheriff. I'll caution you to stick to the facts of the case and not to ask any leading questions. If you do, I'll end this conversation immediately. Are we clear?"

Andy wanted to punch Kent in the face but that would only further complicate things, so he refrained.

"Liddy Lou, can you tell me where you where the night of Macie's murder?"

"I was here."

"The whole evening? You didn't go out at all?"

"Sheriff, I'll caution you not to badger my client. If she says she was here, you should take her statement as fact unless you have evidence to the contrary."

Liddy Lou gave Kent an annoyed look and turned toward Andy to answer for herself.

"Yes, I was here the whole evening."

Andy was shocked. Liddy Lou had just lied to him.

"Just to clarify, we're talking about this past Friday, the tenth. You're certain you didn't go out at all? Is there anyone who can confirm that for you?"

Liddy Lou was no longer looking at him directly when she answered. Her eyes were focused on her lap where she had a string of beads in her hands that she kept rolling between her fingers as she spoke.

"I'm certain I was here the whole evening of the tenth, but I was alone in my room which means no one can confirm my whereabouts for you."

Andy swore under his breath.

"Okay, let me ask this another way. Is there any chance you may have left here, even for a short while, that evening and just don't remember?"

Liddy Lou's eyes remained fixed on her lap and she was about to say something when Kent cut in.

"Sheriff, why do you keep harping on this subject? My client said she was here. Now let's move on to your next question, please."

"Okay, I'll move on, but if you remember anything or you want to go back and add any detail to my first question, just let me know.

"After your run-in with Macie at the Castle Creek Diner, did you have any verbal or written contact or communication of any type with Macie in the days leading up to her death?"

"No, sir, I had no reason to do so."

"So you didn't go see Macie or send her any messages or packages at home or at the studio, then?"

"No, I most certainly did not."

"Who would have access to the welcome baskets you distribute to your guests here at the Inn?"

This question seemed to rattle both Liddy Lou and Kent, who cut Liddy Lou off before she could say anything.

"Sheriff, I'm not sure I understand where you're going with this, so you had better have some type of evidentiary reason or I'm going to shut this whole interrogation down right now."

Andy had been working hard to stay civil, but Kent was working his last nerve, and Liddy Lou lying to him wasn't helping. At this point he needed to take control of this conversation, even if it caused some hurt feelings with the Blocks.

"Look, Kent, I am not interrogating your client yet. I'm asking her questions about her actions and whereabouts on the days leading up to Macie Dixon's murder. I am well within the scope of the law in doing so, and if I don't start getting some straight answers from her, and some cooperation from you, I'm going to be left with no choice but to take her in as a suspect and proceed with an actual interrogation. The choice is up to you, so make your decision and let's get on with this."

Liddy Lou's eyes were as wide as saucers and filling with tears, and it broke Andy's heart.

Kent looked at her and patted her shoulder.

"Sheriff, at this point I feel it's in my client's best interest if we answered no further questions. I strongly believe you have no evidence on which to charge my client, or you would have already done so. However, if you'd like to officially charge my client, then please feel free to arrest her, mirandize her, and continue this conversation at your station."

Liddy Lou was looking at Kent like he'd just grown a second head and started speaking in tongues.

Andy was a damn fine poker player and he knew a bluff call when he heard one. Kent was trying to force him to admit he didn't have enough evidence to charge Liddy Lou. This was one time Andy wished Kent was right.

"You sure this is how you want to play this, Kent?"

"Yes, Sheriff, I am."

Andy stood and looked down at Liddy Lou, who was now squirming in her seat.

"Liddy Lou, look at me, please. I don't doubt Kent is doing what he thinks is best for you but I'm going to ask you to think this through and do what your heart tells you is right here. If there's something you aren't telling me, you need to speak up now or I'm going to be forced to do something I really don't want to do. We both know what you've told me isn't true, and I can't for the life of me understand why you're not being straight with me. If you're afraid of someone, or you're protecting someone, I can help you."

Kent stood up and stepped between Liddy Lou and Andy.

"Okay, Sheriff, that's enough. I will not allow you to berate my client in her own home."

"Kent, sit down and shut up. Your guard-dogging isn't helping Liddy Lou one bit. I know you think I'm bluffing but I'm not, and if Liddy Lou insists on sticking with her current story, I'm going to have to take her in."

"You wouldn't dare," said a familiar voice from the doorway.

Andy turned to see Q'Bita in the doorway, her face a mixture of shock and outrage.

"Q'Bita, she's not giving me much choice."

"Just because Macie was killed with strychnine doesn't mean Nana is guilty. Half the farms in the county still use it for pest control. It could have come from any number of places."

"That's not the only thing I'm basing this on, Q'Bita."

Finally, Liddy Lou rose from her chair and clapped her hands together so loudly it got everyone's attention.

"Enough. I'll have no more bickering over this. Sheriff, I've said all I intend to say without discussing this further with my family and my attorney. If that's an issue, then you do what you have to do."

"Ah, damn it, Liddy Lou, please don't make me do this," Andy pleaded, but Liddy Lou stood still as a statue.

"Liddy Lou Cormier, you are under arrest for the murder of Macie Dixon. You have the right to remain silent. Anything you say can and will be used against you in a court of law. You have the right to an attorney. If you cannot afford an attorney, one will be appointed to you by the court."

Andy continued reading Liddy Lou her rights until Liddy Lou confirmed her understanding. She extended her wrists towards him as if she expected him to slap cuffs on her.

Andy heard Q'Bita gasp and knew he'd just pushed what was left of their relationship over the edge. It was only a matter of time until it reached the bottom and shattered into a million pieces.

"No, Liddy Lou, that isn't necessary. You're not a hardened felon. Let's just take a ride downtown and try to sort this all out, okay? Kent and your family can meet us there."

"I want to go with you."

"Q'Bita, please understand, if there was any way I could let you ride along, I would, but we have a relationship, and because of that I have to play this one by the rules. I can't get to the bottom of this if I'm tied up defending my decisions to every gossip in town who thinks I let my feelings for you taint this investigation."

"He's right, Q'Bita," Kent said.

"Q'Bita, darling, can you please bring my purse and my blood pressure medicine with you to the station? Oh, and my bible, as well? I'm sure the good Lord and I will be having a serious chat at some point soon."

Liddy Lou gave Q'Bita a big hug and turned to face Andy.

"Ready when you are, Sheriff."

The walk to his cruiser was the longest walk of Andy's life. He'd done damage today he wasn't sure he'd be able to ever undo. Most days he loved his job but today wasn't one of those days.

Chapter 26

Liddy Lou had only been arrested two days ago and already the Castle Creek gossip mill was churning at full speed. Nosiness and morbid curiosity resulted in sold-out classes for the next month. Tonight's class was completely full, and there was a waiting list as long as Q'Bita's arm. She had considered canceling this week's classes until she realized it would be to her advantage to keep these people close.

She scanned the room as the last of the participants shuffled in. As usual, some went right to their seats while others helped themselves to snacks, drinks, and the latest tidbits of dirty laundry.

Q'Bita was not surprised to see the queen mother of gossip, Hilde Sanders, working the crowd like a grapevine and stirring up a stew of gossip. Hilde annoyed Q'Bita's nana to no end, but Q'Bita found Hilde's overwhelming need to gossip kind of amusing. Except for tonight. Tonight it was annoying, because her nana was the main topic of conversation.

Evie Newsome was manning the check-in table and gave the signal that all the participants had arrived, and class could start. Q'Bita took a deep breath, flipped on her mic, and jumped in with both feet.

"Hello, folks. Can I have your attention for a few minutes while I do some introductions and cover our safety reminders?"

Most of the group moved towards their seats while a few finished getting refreshments, but there was one small knot of ladies still clustered around Hilde Sanders at the coffee and tea station. Q'Bita was about to break it up when she saw Evie waddle towards them like a mad goose. Hilde must has noticed it, too, because she stepped forward just as Evie reached them and wrapped Evie in a huge hug.

"Oh, Evie, this whole mess with Liddy Lou and Macie is just terrible, isn't it?"

Q'Bita watched in amusement as Evie tried to wriggle free of Hilde's embrace. Evie was barely five feet and weighed less than a hundred pounds. Hilde had at least eight inches and one hundred and fifty pounds on Evie. It looked like a wrestling match between a kitten and a Kodiak bear.

"Put me down, you—"

Evie had been prickly as a hedgehog since Liddy Lou's arrest, and Q'Bita was afraid the kitten might eat the bear if she didn't break this up.

"Okay, ladies, it's time to get started. Who's ready? We'll take a break once everything is in the oven, and we can chat and catch up then."

Hilde let go, and Evie forced her scowl into a smile as she made her way to the front of the room.

Q'Bita went through the usual—introductions, announcements, safety precautions—and was just about to go over the menu when Hilde spoke up.

"Where's Liddy Lou? We can't start without her. We all love her stories about your family's wedding books, and I was hoping she had an update on when her cookbook would be released."

Q'Bita glanced down and saw Evie's hands where balled into fists. She could sense Evie was close to her boiling point again.

"Thank you for asking, Hilde. Liddy Lou sends her regards to all of you but unfortunately she will not be able to join us this evening."

A murmur rippled through the participants and Q'Bita was glad she couldn't make out what they were saying, and extremely glad Evie couldn't, either. She needed Evie to put a cork in her temper long enough to stick to the plan. Q'Bita hadn't spoken to Andy since he'd arrested her nana, and the only way she was going to find the real killer was to find out what Andy knew. Working the gossip mill was the best option she had right now.

Most of these ladies had known Evie Newsome their whole lives and would tell her things they would never tell Q'Bita, whom they still viewed as an outsider.

To Q'Bita's relief, the cooking part of the class went smoothly. As they started break, Q'Bita switched off her mic and pulled Evie aside.

"Are you sure you're up to this, Evie?"

"Yes, I'm fine. I just need to focus and stop letting Hilde get under my skin. That woman sure can bristle my brisket, though. You know she doesn't give a baboon's bunghole about those wedding book stories, and she knows exactly where your nana is. She just wanted to draw attention to Liddy Lou's absence, so she could have something to cackle about with the rest of her brood."

"Yes, I know, and for once that's exactly what we want them to do. Until Judge Tanner gets back from his fishing trip and sets bail, Nana is stuck in jail and can't tell us anything.

Kent says Andy's been keeping everything to himself for now because it's an ongoing investigation, which means we need to figure this out for ourselves. These ladies know everything that goes on in this town, and I need to know what this supposed evidence is so I can get to the bottom of this whole mess and find out who really killed Macie Dixon."

"Well, then, I guess we'd better go work the crowd and see what they know. You take Hilde, though. I just can't."

Evie walked away before Q'Bita could argue.

Q'Bita spotted Hilde holding court with some of her hens near the snacks, and quickly made her way around the other side of the room without being noticed. She snuck in behind them and pretended to organize and restock the snacks while she eavesdropped.

"Well, I'm not sure, either, but I was at the Chamber of Commerce meeting last night and overheard Sammie Hake telling Herschel Vance that Sheriff Hansen and his deputies questioned her. Something about a basket. I got the impression Herschel must also have been questioned."

As Hilde continued, Q'Bita chided herself for avoiding the Chamber of Commerce meeting. If she was going to find the real killer, she needed to get out of the Red Herring Inn and be more social, even if it meant having a few awkward conversations about her nana. The rest of the class went smoothly, and Q'Bita was relieved when it ended without an altercation between Evie and Hilde.

Evie looked tired, so Q'Bita sent her home as soon as class ended. It was almost 9:30 as she loaded the last of the dishes into the dishwasher and heard an incoming text message ping on her phone. She wondered who was texting her this late at night.

She picked up the phone and was surprised to see it was Andy.

"I know you're not happy with me right now, but I thought you should know that Max Tanner just got back from his fishing trip. I asked him to do me a solid and set bail so Liddy Lou can get home. I figured it was best to jump on him before Red got to him. I'll be here at the station if Kent wants to come in and get this taken care of. I hope you know how sorry I am for all of this."

Andy's last sentence slammed into Q'Bita's heart like a meat tenderizer on cube steak, all bumpy and jagged, leaving behind a hundred little holes trying to pull back together what would never fully mend.

Part of her was angry at herself for being so hard on him when he was just doing his job, but the rest of her felt betrayed and was still furious with him for arresting her nana. That part was winning and was not ready to forgive him yet.

"Thank you. I'll call Kent and have him come down."

Q'Bita knew her reply sounded terse and ungrateful but right now she couldn't worry about how she came across. She needed to get Liddy Lou home and come up with a plan to find the real killer.

Chapter 27

Liddy Lou had never been so happy to see her own bed. Andy had done his best to make her comfortable during her stay at the sheriff's station, but the bunk was hard, even with a mattress, and her left hip was killing her. The only thing she wanted when she arrived back at the Red Herring Inn was to take a bath and get some sleep, but Q'Bita had a fresh pot of tea waiting for her. She loved her family and didn't have the heart to brush them off, so she had a quick cup, answered what felt like a hundred questions, and then headed straight for her suite.

It was after midnight when she finally lay down, and all she wanted was to sink into a deep sleep and forget all about the events of the last few days.

It felt like she'd only been asleep for a few minutes when the sound of a ringing phone woke her. A quick glance at the clock on her night stand jolted her upright. It was 9:30 in the morning. She'd never slept past 6 AM a day in her life. Maybe it was true that jail changed a person, she thought to herself and then giggled out loud.

"Hello, Evie," Liddy Lou said, expecting Evie to marvel at how she knew it was her calling. They went through this routine every time Evie called her house phone.

"Is this Liddy Lou Cormier?" asked a male voice that sounded vaguely familiar, but she couldn't quite place.

"Yes."

"Ms. Cormier, this is Spenser Penn from the Castle Creek Gazette. I'd like a few minutes of your time if you're free."

"No comment."

The phone was half-way to hung up when Spenser's voice grew louder.

"It's about your husband so you may want to hear me out."

This was the last thing she'd expected to hear. She hesitated as a thousand thoughts and memories wrestled for space in her mind.

"Ms. Cormier, are you still there?"

"Yes, I'm here, but I have no desire to discuss my late husband or any other matter with you so please do not contact me or my family again. Anything you have to say should be directed to my attorney, Kent Haskell."

"So you have no issue, then, with Mr. Haskell speaking to me about the circumstances surrounding the murder of your husband and questionable suicide of Eliza La Fontaine? As your attorney, I'm assuming he's aware of the fact that you were the main suspect in both those cases. I'm certain my readers will be fascinated to learn Macie Dixon isn't the first person to land on your bad side and end up poisoned."

Liddy Lou couldn't get enough air. It felt like an elephant was sitting on her chest, and her heart was beating so fast it sounded like bongo drums in her ears.

"Mr. Penn, I don't know what you're playing at, and furthermore, I don't care, but let's be clear on one thing: If a single word of what you've just said appears in that rag you call a paper, I'll sue you until the good Lord comes to claim you."

"You'll excuse me if I don't sound wrought with fright, but it's very hard to sue me from prison. This kind of a bombshell has a direct bearing on your case, and the good people of Castle Creek deserve to know the full story. I wouldn't be doing my job if I didn't inform them. It's certainly up to you if you wish to have your side of the story shared or not."

Liddy Lou wanted to jump through the phone and throttle Spenser Penn, but she was already in enough trouble for two people as it was.

"I've said all I care to say. Good day, Mr. Penn."

Liddy Lou hung up the phone before Spenser could reply. She flopped back down in the bed and pulled the blankets over her head.

Chapter 28

The smell of rosemary and lavender permeated the kitchen as Q'Bita minced the herbs she'd picked that morning and tossed them into the chicken salad. Herbed chicken salad was her go-to recipe when she wanted to impress the Inn's guests. It also gave her an excuse to use the imported French cornichons she'd been hoarding.

Pickles of any type were her weakness but cornichons were her favorite. Some women swooned at the sight of a handsome, muscular man but Q'Bita melted at the sight of brined cucumbers. Sometimes she worried about her obsession with food, but when she did she usually just grabbed a jar of pickles and gorged herself until she got over it.

She gave the chicken salad a stir, then snagged a spoonful to check the seasoning. It was perfect; she'd outdone herself with this batch. She just hoped her lunch guest wouldn't be so busy eating she'd fail to share anything useful.

During Liddy Lou's two-day stay at the Castle Creek Sheriff's department, she'd managed to pick up some useful information about the case. When she arrived back home last night, she'd filled them in on everything she'd overheard. Q'Bita was surprised to hear that in the days leading up to Macie Dixon's murder she and her assistant, Hadleigh Banks, had a huge falling out.

Q'Bita couldn't help wondering what this falling out was all about and whether it could be a motive for murder. After her nana went to bed, it didn't take long for Q'Bita to convince Jamie they needed to get to know Hadleigh Banks a little better and see what they could find out about this argument.

It was Jamie's idea to invite Hadleigh to lunch at the Red Herring Inn. Q'Bita agreed it was a great idea, but she also suspected Jamie might have ulterior motives since he'd already let slip that he was attracted to Hadleigh.

Jamie was cute in a dorky sort of way, and if it happened to work to their advantage, then Q'Bita was fine with it, unless, of course, Hadleigh Banks really was a murderer, in which case she'd need to keep Jamie as far from Hadleigh as possible.

Q'Bita stopped, popped a cornichon in her mouth, and tried to relax. She was getting all worked up and needed to focus. She was just starting to feel calm and focused again when she heard Rene's voice outside.

"Now remember, Rolfie, once we're inside you can't shed a single piece of fur. Q'Bita and Liddy Lou have a strict no-cats-allowed-in-the-cooking-school policy. They're terrible people, and if they suspect you've been in here they'll lock up the crème fraiche, and we'll both have to resort to using milk. Unconscionable, I know, but that's just how these country folks are."

Q'Bita laughed as she opened the screen door to let them in.

"Luckily for you both, my brother is more attracted to sarcasm then subtlety."

She gave Rolfie a quick scratch between the ears and Rene a smack on the arm.

"Nana and I are not terrible people, or cat haters. You know full well Culinary Forensics is considered a food business and the Department of Health doesn't allow animals in the kitchen."

"Hmm, interesting. I see Evie in here all the time, and she's definitely part goat."

"I'm going to tell her you said that."

"Don't you dare! She'll lure me into the oven with candy and then turn me into that jerky she's obsessed with. Not that I wouldn't be delicious, because we both know I would be."

Q'Bita placed a bowl of cream on the floor, and Rolfie began to devour it as if he hadn't eaten in days.

"Why does it smell like pine and soap in here?"

"Hadleigh Banks is coming over for lunch. This is her first visit to the Red Herring Inn, so I made my famous herbed chicken salad."

"Umm, and you're just telling me this now, because… Why? Do you have any idea how long it takes me to pull all this together? Your chicken salad is tasty, but it's only going to get us so far. We'll need my dazzling charm and good looks to seal the deal, which means I'll need to bring my most stylish A-game to this soirée."

"No offense, but I was planning on using Jamie as the man candy for this one. You're welcome to join us but you need to promise me you'll dial it down a notch. It's more of a friendly get-to-know-you lunch than an interrogation session. We're just going to chat and hopefully learn what Hadleigh and Macie were arguing about. And before you ask, no, we won't be waterboarding her for dessert."

"Okay, suit yourself. I personally love ending a good meal with a little kink, but I guess it's not for everyone."

Rolfie had finished his saucer of cream and was now cleaning his paws and ignoring them both. Rene bent over and scooped him up like he was carrying a baby.

"Come, puss-ums. Papa has to go channel his inner Jessica Fletcher and get back here before Q'Bita and Jamie muck up this whole investigation. I swear I'm the glue that holds this whole dysfunctional family together most days."

Rene pivoted like a ballerina and flounced out of the kitchen with a small wave over his shoulder and a snarky comment about being back shortly so they could get properly prepared.

Jamie arrived a few minutes later, as Q'Bita was taking the shortbread crust out of the oven.

"What's shaking, Q'B-doll?"

She gave him a wave on her way to the walk-in, where she stowed the crusts to cool. She grabbed the ingredients for her tart filling and asked Jamie to put on the kettle for tea.

117

"Q'Bita, it's 80 degrees out. How can you drink hot tea?"

"The tea is for the tart filling, not for us. I'm making a Lady Gray cream tart for dessert. I thought it would go well with the rosemary and lavender in the chicken salad."

"I hope you put as much thought into how we're going to get Hadleigh to spill her guts as you have the menu."

"Spill her guts about what?" asked Liddy Lou as she entered the kitchen from the dining room. You two had better not be up to something."

Jamie and Q'Bita exchanged guilty looks, and Liddy Lou grunted in disgust.

"Q'Bita Colleen Block, I will not stand for this, you hear me? This isn't one of your parents' books. There's a real killer out there, and I've got enough to worry about without having to fret about you two getting yourselves killed next. Both of you need to stay out of this and leave the investigating to the professionals."

Jamie gulped so loud Q'Bita could hear it half-way across the kitchen. She scolded herself for being so careless. She hadn't even considered that the killer might target one of them if they got too close.

"Well, this is just great. Now I've forgotten what I came in here for in the first place."

Liddy Lou turned and walked back out the same way she'd come in.

"Awkward much?" Jamie said.

"Ugh, I hate upsetting her, but someone needs to get this whole mess figured out, and it doesn't look like Andy is making much progress."

"Speaking of awkward, how's things between you and the law man?"

Q'Bita didn't want to talk about Andy or even think about how strained things were between them right now.

"Things have been better but I'm sure we'll manage to work it out after he arrests the real killer and clears Nana of any wrongdoing."

Q'Bita filled the tarts and popped them into the oven just as Rene returned. As she cleaned up, Rene and Jamie were busy brainstorming their master plan to entrap Hadleigh. Obviously, they'd both been reading too many of her parents' books.

"Okay, you two, let's bring it down a notch for a minute. We don't even know if Hadleigh's done anything wrong. We certainly don't know enough yet to start assuming she's the killer."

The sound of tires crunching on the gravel interrupted their conversation.

"Okay, that has to be her. Both of you need to stay calm and follow my lead. I'm the only one who has acting experience, and this little charade is going to require a professional."

"Tell me again why he's here," Jamie asked.

Q'Bita met Hadleigh at the side door.

"Hi, Hadleigh. It's nice to finally meet you in person. Come on in and I'll introduce you."

Hadleigh gave Q'Bita a meek smile and stepped inside Culinary Forensics. Her eyes grew wider as she looked around.

"Wow, this place is amazing. It must be fabulous getting to spend the whole day cooking here."

Rene made a noise that sounded like a cross between a cough and a sputter.

"Yoo-hoo! Hello."

He waived with his whole arm, as if he was trying to signal a landing plane. Q'Bita wasn't sure if she should cringe or laugh. She noticed Jamie was glaring at Rene and looked like he was about to choke him.

Hadleigh took a step towards Jamie and Rene.

"You must be Rene. Nice to meet you. I've heard a lot about you."

"I bet you have," Jamie blurted with no attempt to disguise his sarcasm.

Hadleigh blushed, turning towards Jamie but not making eye

contact.

"You must be Jamie."

"Hmm, notice she didn't say it was nice to meet you or that she's heard about you. Must mean she doesn't have anything nice to say. Doesn't surprise me, really."

Q'Bita realized things were starting to spiral out of control and wondered why she hadn't just handled this herself. If Jamie and Rene kept bickering, Hadleigh wasn't going to get a chance to tell them anything useful.

"Okay, boys, let's play nice."

Jamie shot Rene a look and then turned to Hadleigh and smiled.

"Don't pay any attention to him. He gets hangry when we don't feed him every two hours."

"He's lying. I am always perfectly civil, I assure you. He just lacks the sophistication necessary to appreciate my witty banter."

"God, you're an ass," Jamie replied.

Q'Bita couldn't watch this another second.

"Hadleigh, would you like to see the rest of the Red Herring? I'd love to show you our grounds; they're beautiful at this time of year."

"That sounds lovely. Will Jamie and Rene be joining us?"

Q'Bita quickly blurted out, "No." Jamie and Rene looked offended. "The guys are going to stay back and finish getting lunch set up on the deck for us. Everything is in the fridge. We won't be long, guys."

Q'Bita led Hadleigh outside towards the kitchen herb garden.

"This is my favorite spot on the grounds. It was a welcome-home present from my brother Beecher and Rene. It reminds me of the garden my husband Alain gave me in Spain."

"Macie told me your husband was killed in a traffic accident. I can't imagine how hard it must be to lose someone you love so suddenly like that."

A twinge of guilt ran through Q'Bita. Hadleigh seemed like a genuinely nice person, and she hated trying to manipulate her for information. It just seemed so hard to believe the girl standing in front of her could be a cold-blooded killer.

"Some days are harder than others but fortunately I have my family and friends to help me through the tough days."

Hadleigh looked down at the ground, and Q'Bita could see tears welling in the corners of her eyes.

"Oh gosh, I'm sorry. I'm being insensitive. You've had a terrible loss yourself recently, and I haven't even asked you how you're doing."

Hadleigh wiped at her eyes with the back of her hand and let out a little chuckle.

"Sorry, just laughing at the irony of all this. I was worried about coming here today. I wondered why you invited me, since I can't imagine you or your family wanting anything to do with the Dixons at this point. Yet you're the only person to even bother asking me how I'm doing. Macie's own family doesn't even seem to care. It's like they've forgotten I even exist."

Her words carried so much sadness Q'Bita couldn't stop herself from reaching out and wrapping Hadleigh in a big hug. Hadleigh stiffened at first but then relaxed and sniffled on Q'Bita's shoulder. Q'Bita kept at it for a few more seconds then let go.

"Sorry, I'm a hugger; I can't help myself."

Hadleigh wiped at her tears again and then smiled at Q'Bita.

"No problem. I really needed a hug. My family isn't much for hugging or feelings, really."

By the time they'd finished their tour of the grounds Rene and Jamie had lunch ready on the back patio. Lunch went smoothly, with everyone making pleasant small talk, and it seemed like Hadleigh was feeling comfortable talking to them.

Q'Bita excused herself to go plate dessert and was thrilled when Hadleigh insisted on helping. It might work to her advantage to get Hadleigh alone for a few minutes and see if she could get her to talk about the argument with Macie.

"Wow, Q'Bita, I really can't get over how amazing your kitchen is. It's no wonder people love taking cooking classes here. I'd kill to have a place like this."

A tickle ran down Q'Bita's spine as Hadleigh's words sank in. Could it be possible Hadleigh meant that literally? Maybe the argument was work-related and had ended in Hadleigh killing Macie.

"Thanks. We're lucky. Owning the Red Herring Inn means we can live together as a family and make a living doing what each of us really loves doing. Life doesn't get much better than that. Did you help Macie much with the cooking on the show?"

"Me? Oh gosh, no. I can't cook any better than Macie could. That's why she had Patti Becker."

"Speaking of Patti, I hope it's okay to ask you this… I figure if anyone knows the truth, it would probably be you. Is there any truth to the rumors that Patti put poison in Macie's food?"

"From what I gather, it's true. Patti claims she only meant to make Macie sick, and apparently it wasn't what killed Macie. Aren't you dating the sheriff? I thought he would have told you about the case."

"Thank you, Jesus," Q'Bita muttered to herself. This was exactly the opening she'd been hoping for.

"Because my nana has been charged with Macie's murder Andy can't tell me or my family anything. It's frustrating. I don't care what the evidence says, my nana didn't kill Macie, but the Dixons seem convinced she did. I'm afraid if I don't do something to get to the bottom of this my nana might end up going to jail for something she didn't do. I've heard rumors you and Macie had a falling-out a few days before her murder. Would you tell me what it was about? It might not have anything at all to do with the case, but if there's any chance it does, then anything you can tell me might help clear my nana."

Hadleigh looked like a rabbit who'd been cornered by a hawk, and Q'Bita was worried she might have blown it, until Hadleigh pulled out a stool and sat down.

"We did have an argument. Macie caught me snooping in her office and accused me of trying to sabotage her. She could be a little dramatic at times. Things were said by both of us that weren't nice, and she fired me."

"Macie fired you? You must have been furious."

"Not really. By nature, I'm a very honest person, and let's just say the Dixons don't always play by the rules. I'd reached a point where I couldn't stay in that environment."

"Wow, was that the last time you talked to Macie before… well, you know?"

"You mean before she died? It wasn't the last time. The day she died I was gathering my things from the TV Studio when Macie came in and apologized. We had a long talk and she explained why she was the way she was, and I believe she was sincere. Macie was a product of her upbringing, but she wasn't all bad, just spoiled and misguided. She told me she was tired of the way people perceived her and was ready to change, which is another reason why I came here today."

This last comment caught Q'Bita completely off guard.

"I'm not sure I understand. Why here?"

Hadleigh got up and grabbed her purse off the hook near the door. She reached inside, pulled out a file folder of loose pages, and handed them to Q'Bita. Q'Bita opened the folder and was shocked to see it was full of copies of her nana's recipes.

"Where did you get these?"

"That's what I found when Macie caught me snooping in her office. Macie didn't take them, but she certainly didn't refuse them when they were offered. It's what we argued about. The day she died she explained the whole situation to me and asked me to reconsider leaving. I agreed to stay on the condition she bring these back to your nana, apologize, then start over clean. I guess she never got the chance."

This should have been great news, but instead it made Q'Bita's heart sink. On one hand it proved her nana had been right to accuse

Macie of using her recipes, but on the other hand it gave Liddy Lou an even stronger motive to kill Macie.

Q'Bita forced herself to focus but it wasn't easy.

"Wait. You said Macie didn't take these. How do you know that's true?"

"She got them from someone named Tony. He gave them to her and then kept coming around telling Macie she owed him and needed to settle up. I got the impression Macie didn't care much for him and was maybe even a little afraid of him."

"Did you tell this to the sheriff? Do you know this Tony's last name?"

Hadleigh squirmed nervously on the stool.

"No, I didn't. I'm afraid if I tell them about Tony I'll have to tell them about arguing with Macie and they'll think I killed her. I was hoping you might be able to help me figure out how to tell them since the sheriff is your boyfriend. I don't believe your grandmother killed Macie, and I swear I didn't do it, but it's possible this Tony guy had something to do with it."

Q'Bita didn't know what to think. Either Hadleigh Banks was the best actress she'd ever met, or she'd just cracked this case wide open. Either way, Q'Bita needed to talk to Andy as soon as possible. She was glad she'd made two pies, since she hadn't exactly been nice to Andy recently, and he'd already confessed pie was the way to his heart.

Chapter 29

Q'Bita's hands were shaking as she pressed the send button to call Andy. What if he was still angry and didn't pick up? What if he got even more angry at her for talking to Hadleigh? Andy answered before the first ring ended, and it caught her off guard.

"Hey there. Were your ears ringing? I was just thinking about giving you a call."

"Maybe you just sensed I had extra pie and you couldn't resist."

"I did not pick up on the pie vibes, but now that it's been brought to my attention I may need to investigate."

"I'd like that."

Andy was quiet for a second then cleared his throat.

"I have some information to share but you're probably not going to like it."

"Well, I have some to share with you, too, so maybe we should just discuss everything over pie."

"Man, I was hoping you'd say that. I'm leaving the station now."

Q'Bita was relieved when Andy greeted her with a hug. It felt good to be in his arms again even if it was only for a few seconds. She missed him and hated what this mess was doing to their relationship.

They exchanged small talk while Andy made his way through the first round of pie.

"So, I told you there was something I wanted to share with you. Promise me you won't get upset, okay?"

"Only if you make me the same promise."

"Deal. I've heard some grumbling that Red's calling in favors trying to get the trial date moved up. It looks like he's going to get his way, too. I can't tell Kent without getting my ass in hot water, and you can't tell him where you found out, but someone needs to make sure he knows about this and is ready to push back."

"Does this mean you still don't have any other suspects?"

"I'm sorry, sweetheart. I'm trying everything I can, I promise."

"I know you are, and I just might be able to help you with that."

Andy dropped his fork and sat up straight.

"Q'Bita, please tell me you haven't been messing with this investigation. If we're right and Liddy Lou is being set up, that means there's someone else out there who has killed once and won't hesitate to do it again."

"There's no if, Andy. We are right. My nana didn't do this, but I have an idea who might have."

"Who?"

"Hadleigh Banks was here for lunch today, and she brought me these." Q'Bita pushed the file folder of recipes towards Andy. "These are photocopies of my nana's recipes. Hadleigh found them in a safe in Macie's office. When she asked about them Macie admitted they were stolen. She got them from someone named Tony. Hadleigh doesn't know Tony's last name but she said he's come around a few times and she can give you a description. Tony had been pestering Macie about owing him and needing to settle up. Hadleigh also claims Macie had a change of heart and was going to return the recipes to my nana the day she died. We need to find out who this Tony is. He might be our killer."

"She told you all this? Did it occur to you she might be lying? Both Chance and I interviewed her, and she never once mentioned any of this to us."

"I know. She told me that, too. She's afraid if she tells you, you might think she killed Macie."

"Okay. I'll bring her in to get a description then start looking into this Tony guy, but promise me you'll stop playing detective. I couldn't take it if anything happened to you. Besides, I can't concentrate if I'm distracted worrying about you."

Three slices of pie and half a pitcher of sweet tea called for a walk. Q'Bita was glad she'd called him, and by the time he left it felt like things were better between them. She just hoped they stayed that way.

After Andy left, Q'Bita filled her family in about Tony and the possibility of Red moving up the trial. Her father called Kent Haskell, who promised to address the trial date issue with the judge ASAP.

Long after the others had gone to bed, Q'Bita noticed her nana sitting by the fire in the library. Liddy Lou had been very calm and quiet through their whole discussion, and that wasn't like her at all. Something had changed since her nana came home, and Q'Bita was worried about her.

Q'Bita knelled down next to her nana's chair and put her arm around her shoulders.

"Nana, is there anything you want to talk about? You haven't seemed yourself the last few days."

Liddy Lou shook her head and patted Q'Bita on the shoulder.

"No, dear, I'm fine. Just tired from all the drama we've had."

Q'Bita kissed her nana on the top of the head.

"If you insist, I'll let it go, but just know that I'm here if you need to talk, Nana."

A sad look flitted across her nana's face, and a wave of foreboding washed over Q'Bita.

***

Q'Bita was the early riser of the family, which meant she was also the coffee maker, but today someone had beaten her to it. The smell of fresh coffee pulled her from her bed and drew her to the kitchen. Her parents sat drinking coffee with her nana. Tension hung in the room and gave Q'Bita an uneasy feeling.

"It's too early for any of you to be up. What's going on?"

"Kent spoke to Judge Tanner last night, and the judge informed him that given the circumstances he saw no reason not to grant Red

Dixon's request for an escalated trial."

Her father looked directly at her nana when he said circumstances.

"Okay, I'm confused. What circumstances is he referring to?"

Both her parents were now looking at her nana the way they used to look at her or Beecher when they'd done something wrong and were expected to explain themselves.

The sound of the side door opening broke the tension in the room. Jamie took one step inside and stopped abruptly.

"Did I just interrupt something? You all look way too serious for this early in the morning."

"Tom," said Liddy Lou, "now that Jamie's here maybe you should go wake Beecher and Rene. It's probably best if I just get everything out in the open all at once."

Q'Bita had no idea what her nana was about to tell them, but she was sure she wasn't going to like it. She grabbed four more coffee cups and started another pot while they waited for Beecher and Rene to join them. Then she grabbed a tray of scones from the walk-in and popped them in the oven to warm through.

Liddy Lou looked at her assembled family and took a deep breath.

"I know this is upsetting for all of you, but I fear I've brought some of this on myself. Please understand I wasn't trying to hide anything or lie to any of you. I've been trying to protect you. What you don't know you can't be forced to tell. There's a few things I've been keeping to myself that in hind sight I should have shared with the sheriff, and those things are now biting me in the butt."

Liddy Lou's hands were shaking as she took a sip of coffee and reached for a scone.

"Good Lord, woman, don't stop now. You tore me from the depths of my beauty sleep for this, so let's hear it. Besides, those scones aren't the least bit juicy, and I'm guessing this story is."

Beecher put a hand on Rene's arm and made a zipping motion across his lips.

"The sheriff is in possession of security tapes from the TV station, which I didn't know existed when he was here speaking with Kent and myself. Had I known this, I might have chosen to be more forthcoming. These tapes show me entering the TV station on the day Macie died, which, as you know, contradicts what I told the sheriff, and that's why he thinks I'm lying to him."

"Wait. You were at the TV Station that day? Why?" asked Q'Bita.

"This ridiculous argument had gotten completely out of control, and I was hoping if I took the high road and reached out to her in a friendly, civil way then maybe we could resolve this whole mess, but I never got the chance. Right after I got to the TV Station the power went out, and I left. I spent the next few hours walking around, which means I have no alibi."

"Okay, I agree that looks pretty bad, but that can't possibly be enough to warrant escalating a trial date, can it?" Beecher asked.

Kari Block reached across the table and held her mother's hand.

"Why don't you get another cup of coffee? I can tell them the rest, Mama."

"If you don't mind, I think I'm going to step outside and pluck some fresh chamomile. I could use a nice cup of tea."

Q'Bita put on a kettle of water and then returned to the table.

Kari dabbed at the corners of eyes with a tissue and blew her nose, sounding like a fog horn.

"I don't talk much about my father, mostly because it hurts your nana, but there are some things about his death that directly impact your nana's case. These things are about to become public knowledge, and I want to tell you about it before you read the Spenser Penn version."

"I thought Papa was killed in a robbery. How does that impact Nana?" Beecher asked.

"Well, that's the story that made it to the papers but there's more to it than that. It's true my father was shot in the parking lot of a motel, but the local police were convinced it was just staged to look like a robbery. The part that isn't common knowledge is that my father wasn't the only person found dead that day. He was found just outside a room where our local congressman's wife supposedly committed suicide.

"Her official cause of death was listed as suicide by drug overdose, but the coroner found high levels of strychnine in her system. Witnesses came forward saying they'd seen her and my father together at the motel on several occasions. For a long time after their deaths the police were convinced she and my father were having an affair and your nana killed them out of jealousy. The police could never make the case, and when the congressman decided to run for governor, he wanted the whole mess kept quiet."

They all sat silently for a few seconds letting Kari's words sink in. Finally, Jamie spoke up. "You said this was going to become public knowledge. If Liddy Lou was never charged, can they even bring this up at trial?"

"Once Spenser prints his twisted version of events they won't need to bring it up at trial. Everyone in town will already know about it and will have formed their own opinion, good or bad," explained Tom.

They'd all been so wrapped up in Kari's story they hadn't noticed Liddy Lou was back from the kitchen garden.

"Tom's right. It is going to look really bad for me, but I want all of you to know, I didn't believe your papa was having an affair then, and I still don't believe it now. Those deaths are connected for sure, but I didn't have anything to do with them. If Spenser Penn wants to drag up the past and plaster it all over the front page, then it is what it is, and there's nothing we can do about it. I've decided to put all this in the Lord's hands and have faith he'll see me through it."

They finished their coffee and the rest of the scones. It was only 9:30, and Q'Bita already hated how long this day had been. Jamie stayed to help her load the dishwasher.

"Okay, Q'B-Doll, I can smell the carrots and onions coming out your ears so tell me what's got you stewing."

"Why didn't Andy tell me about the security tapes? He told me about Red wanting to move up the trial date. Why keep the rest from me?"

"I don't know, darling, but whatever his reason, I am sure he didn't do it to hurt you. He cares about you, Q'B-Doll, so don't let all this come between you."

"I'm trying, Jamie, but it's hard. They aren't making any headway in this investigation, and I'm starting to wonder if they will before it's too late."

"Well, maybe they just need our help. I think it's time to have another chat with Hadleigh and see if we can find out more about this Tony person."

Chapter 30

Liddy Lou slapped the morning paper down so hard it caused tea to slosh over the top of her cup. Spenser Penn's article about Henry's murder and Eliza La Fontaine's questionable suicide was splashed all over the front page. He'd done his usual job of polishing a turd till it sparkled like the sun. Liddy Lou just hoped everyone didn't get so blinded by the sparkle they failed to see the shit pile behind the shine.

Her cell phone rang. The caller ID said Private Number, so she let it go to voicemail. After a few seconds the voicemail alert beeped. She took a long sip of tea then pushed the button to listen to the message.

"Good morning, Ms. Cormier. By now I'm sure you've seen today's Castle Creek Gazette. Such unfortunate timing, don't you think? I imagine this article isn't going to help your case. Heck, it just might be the nail in your coffin. I think it's time you and I had a friendly chat about your options. I'll be at the Castle Creek Diner around 10 if you're interested. Feel free to bring Haskell with you if you want, but it would probably go smoother if you just came alone."

Liddy Lou's blood was boiling. She should have guessed that pompous ass Red Dixon was behind Spenser's article. That smug bastard had some nerve calling her up and gloating. She got up and started pacing like a caged cat. Deep down she knew she should ignore the bait, call Kent Haskell, and let him deal with this. On the other hand, this might be the only shot she had to tell Red Dixon to kiss her ass before they threw that ass in prison.

Liddy Lou arrived at the diner a few minutes before 10. Red was already there. He'd taken the liberty of ordering coffee for them both, so she asked Dot to bring her a cup of tea just to be difficult.

"Hello, Liddy Lou. Thank you for coming on such short notice. Can I get you anything to eat?"

"No, I'm fine, thank you."

"Very well. I'm a busy man and have little interest in small talk so why don't we get right to business? Even a hack like Kent Haskell must know you have little chance of acquittal. Spenser's article pretty much ensures that won't happen. You're not a young woman, and you have a family to think about, so I'd like to offer you a deal."

Liddy Lou had heard enough. She stood up to leave.

"I wouldn't be so quick to dismiss me, Liddy Lou. I haven't finished yet, and I think you'll be quite interested in hearing what I have to say."

"I'm a God-fearing woman, Mr. Dixon, and I have no intention of making a deal with the devil, thank you very much."

This made Red laugh. She was sure she wasn't the first person to make the comparison, and probably wouldn't be the last.

"I assure you if I had that kind of power we wouldn't be having this conversation, and there'd be no trial. Now, shall we get back to our discussion?"

Red motioned to the seat she'd previously occupied, and against her better judgment, she sat back down.

"If you plead guilty and waive your right to a trial I will see to it that Judge Tanner gives you two weeks to put your affairs in order and say goodbye to your family and friends. I will also refrain from filing a civil suit against you, which I would likely win, resulting in the forfeiture of all your assets, including the Red Herring Inn, which I believe is still in your name. I'm sure I don't have to tell you how terrible it would be for your family to lose their home and their primary source of income so soon after losing you."

Liddy Lou was stunned. She had already reconciled herself to the fact they were likely going to lose at trial, but it hadn't occurred to her Red Dixon would file a civil suit.

"Let me make this easy for you, Liddy Lou. Why don't you take the rest of the day to think this over, discuss it with Kent, or whomever, and get back to me by noon tomorrow?"

Red pushed back his chair and stood up, casually tossing a twenty-dollar bill on the table to cover their drinks. His arrogance was infuriating.

"Enjoy the rest of your day, Liddy Lou. We'll talk soon."

Dot rushed over as soon as Red was out the door.

"Are you okay, darling? Can I bring you anything? What on earth was that all about?"

Liddy Lou forced a smile and shook her head.

"No, I'm fine, Dot, but thank you for asking. We were just talking business, is all. By any chance, has Kent Haskell been in this morning?"

"Sure, sugar, he's still here. He likes to hide in the back where he can read the paper in peace and quiet."

Liddy Lou finished her tea and fixed her lipstick. The walk to the back of the diner felt like it took days. At her age, she'd slowed down a bit, but today it felt like the soles of her shoes were made of lead. Kent Haskell peered at her over the top of his paper before folding it and placing it on the table in front of him.

"So, I was hoping you'd make your way back here and tell me why you took it upon yourself to meet with Red Dixon without including me."

Liddy Lou raised a hand to stop him, and he offered her a seat.

"Kent, I'm sorry. I thought, well, I don't know what I thought, really. This whole mess is just getting to me. Red has offered me a deal, and I wanted to hear what he had to say."

"Wait. He did what? Please tell me you didn't agree to anything."

"No, I didn't. He presented his offer then gave me until noon tomorrow to make a decision."

As Liddy Lou recounted her conversation with Red, Kent alternated between pale and scarlet.

"Be honest with me, Kent, do you think we have any chance of winning, and can he really file a civil suit?"

Kent was quiet. She could tell he was carefully weighing everything she'd said.

"Liddy Lou, we've known each other a long time, and you know I'll do everything in my power to win this case, but you also know I'm brutally honest."

"It's okay, Kent. I'm a big girl. I can handle the truth."

"I've worried from the beginning about being able to win against Red Dixon. Most of the evidence is circumstantial but there's a lot of it. The security tape is going to kill us, especially if the prosecution introduces the fact that you lied about it. If all that wasn't bad enough, then there's this damn article."

Kent slapped the folder newspaper laying on the table and rolled his eyes.

"I'll fight with you to the gates of hell but if I'm being honest, I can't promise you it will be enough to get a win."

"Since we're being honest, give it to me straight. If I don't take Red's offer, and we lose, can he really take the Red Herring?"

"Absolutely. Judge Tanner is run so far up Red Dixon's ass he'll probably give Red the shirt off your back while you're on the way to jail. And it isn't just if we lose. Red can still go after you in civil court even if we win."

"What? How can that be? If I haven't done anything, and the court finds me innocent, how can he possibly take me to court again?"

"Criminal and civil courts try the same evidence but in completely different ways. Criminal courts determine guilt and dispense punishment based on guilt beyond a reasonable doubt, whereas civil courts are far less strict and seek to compensate victims, or their families, based on the balance of probability. This is where the circumstantial evidence in this case presents a serious problem for you."

"So what I'm hearing is that the only way I can protect my family from losing their home and their livelihood is to take Red's deal."

"I can't tell you what to do, because it's your choice, but I'd be lying if I said our chances of winning were worth the risk. They aren't. Right now, we need a miracle. Let's just hope whoever did this either has a crisis of conscience or the sheriff catches one hell of a break before the trial starts."

Liddy Lou tried to speak but the words were all balled up in her throat. She'd spent every penny she had buying the Red Herring Inn at auction so she could bring her family together and give them a place to heal. Each had their own wounds. Kari and Tom had weathered a cancer scare. Beecher and Rene had been black-listed from finding work on Broadway by Rene's ex, and Q'Bita had lost her husband to a terrible accident.

She loved them all so much, and she couldn't bear putting them through any more than they'd already been through. This wasn't a hard decision. They'd survive without her, but she couldn't ask them to be without a place to call home.

"Let's say I take this deal… how much time am I'm looking at?"

Kent's hands were shaking, and a tear rolled down his cheek.

"Liddy Lou, are you one hundred percent sure you want to go down this road? Even if you take this deal, Judge Tanner isn't going to go easy on you. I'm not trying to be unkind, but even a twenty-year sentence, which isn't out of the question, means you'll…"

His words trailed off in a mumble.

"It means I'll most likely die before I'm even eligible for parole."

"Yes, it's possible."

"I'm okay with that, Kent. I couldn't protect my Henry from whatever it was he got himself messed up in but with the good Lord's help I've been able to do right by my Kari and her family. I have faith God will put me where I need to be when I need to be there, and if that's jail, then that's the plan he has for me."

"I wish I had your conviction of faith, Liddy Lou, because I cannot for the life of me understand how you going to jail for a crime you didn't commit serves a higher purpose."

"Give it time, Kent. Faith strengthens with age, and I have quite a few years on you."

"Well, it sounds like your mind is made up, then. I can request a meeting with Red and his people when you're ready."

"I'm as ready as I'll ever be. I just want to put this behind us so my family can move on."

Chapter 31

Q'Bita sat on the front porch of the Red Herring Inn trying to process all the thoughts racing through her mind. She'd finished calling everyone enrolled in tonight's class to let them know it was being rescheduled and was surprised no one had asked why.

Her nana had stunned the whole family with the news that she'd taken a plea deal, and Q'Bita was relieved the gossip mill hadn't gotten wind of it just yet.

She knew she should be inside trying to comfort her family, but her mother's sobbing was more than she could take. The sound of an approaching vehicle drew her attention. Normally, she'd be happy to see Andy, but he wasn't here to see her this time. This was official business. The terms of her nana's plea deal included house arrest and electronic monitoring for the two weeks until her sentencing.

Andy pulled around to the side parking lot. The less attention they drew the better. Her father had already hung up on Spenser Penn, and it wouldn't be long before the local news station showed up.

Q'Bita walked around the side of the Inn and found Andy getting the monitoring equipment out of his truck. He saw her and stopped.

"Hi, beautiful."

His smile looked more pained then happy.

"Hey."

Andy stepped forward and wrapped her in a hug. She usually turned to mush in his arms but tonight, it just wasn't the same. Andy let go after a few seconds and took a step back.

"I'm so sorry, sweetheart. I cannot understand what possessed your nana to take a plea, but you have my word, I'll keep working this case until I find the truth."

"I appreciate that, Andy, but I'm not sure it will do any good now. I just don't understand why she'd do a thing like this. She's innocent. She says she did it for us but…"

A flood of tears took over her words as Q'Bita buried her face in her hands.

Andy stepped forward and wrapped his arms around her again.

"I know it's hard to believe this right now, but you guys are going to get through this. I promise."

The sound of someone clearing their throat interrupted their hugging.

"Hey, Beecher," Andy said.

"Sheriff. Sorry to interrupt but it's getting late and Nana is tired. I think it's best if we just get this over with so she can turn in."

Beecher helped Andy carry the equipment into the library where the rest of the family was waiting with Kent and Jamie.

Andy adjusted the ankle monitor until it was snug but not uncomfortable and explained how it all worked. Liddy Lou would have the run of the Red Herring Inn and the front porch but no further without express permission of the court.

The ankle monitor was to stay on at all times until she appeared for sentencing, at which time it would be removed under supervision of the court.

Despite Rene's protest in favor of something smaller and more stylish, her nana took the whole process in stride. She seemed to be at peace with her decision, though for the life of her, Q'Bita could not understand how.

One by one her family slowly trickled off to bed, and Jamie and Kent said their goodbyes, leaving Q'Bita and Andy alone in the library.

"There's a full moon tonight. Wanna take a walk and get some air?" Andy asked.

"That sounds wonderful."

As they walked, Q'Bita mustered up the courage to ask Andy where he was with the investigation.

"Honestly, Q'Bita, so far we haven't found a single thing that doesn't point at Liddy Lou. If someone is setting her up, they're doing a damn fine job. I know that wasn't what you wanted to hear but it's all I've got."

"Have you looked into Hadleigh Banks at all? Did you have her come in to give the description of our mystery man, Tony?

"I left her two messages today, but she hasn't called me back."

Q'Bita sighed and kicked at a stone as they walked.

"She seems sweet, but she does have a past record, and she'd recently fought with Macie. We only have her word they made up. I can't put my finger on anything specific, but I got the sense she was holding back and there's more to the story than she shared."

"I ordered a full background check on her right before I left the station. It should be back in a day or two, and we'll see what turns up. If there's even a sliver of something, I will bring her in and question her again."

Q'Bita didn't bother sharing that she and Jamie were planning on doing their own second round of questioning with Hadleigh. She was sure Andy would object and tell her not to investigate on her own, but her nana only had two weeks of freedom left, and she wasn't about to waste a single second letting someone else do the investigating.

***

When Hadleigh'd come for lunch the other day, she'd mentioned twice how nice it would be to cook in a kitchen like Culinary Forensics, which gave them the perfect cover for inviting Hadleigh back over the following day.

Q'Bita called her around nine and asked if she'd like to come help with some recipe testing and then stay for lunch. Hadleigh jumped at the offer and said she'd be there by ten.

Even though it wasn't real, the recipe testing was going quite well. Hadleigh was artistic and had a great eye for detail and plating. They made a few dozen petit fours and tea sandwiches then decided to take an iced tea break on the porch before starting lunch.

Q'Bita phoned the front desk and asked Jamie to take a break and join them.

Hadleigh and Jamie were chatting about comic book villains while Q'Bita sat pretending to listen. She was waiting for a break in the conversation, so she could bring up the mysterious Tony when she heard Rene arguing with someone. The conversation was growing louder as they approached the porch from the side yard.

"I'm telling you, red is all wrong and simply won't do. Savannah Gavin asked for classy, not a bordello of blood. She wants something that says summer in the Hamptons, not Mayan sacrifice."

They rounded the corner and Q'Bita saw Antonio trailing behind Rene, looking annoyed. Rene spotted Q'Bita, Jamie, and Hadleigh on the porch.

"Oh, Q'Bita, there you are. Will you please tell the Latin Libido that red works just fine for the upholstery in his pimp wagon but it—"

The sound of shattering glass caused Rene to stop speaking mid-sentence.

Q'Bita turned towards the sound and saw Hadleigh had dropped her glass on the porch and was staring at Rene and Antonio like she'd seen a ghost.

Jamie jumped up and grabbed a napkin, handing it to Hadleigh. Q'Bita looked back towards Rene and noticed Antonio was walking away.

"You're right, Rene, red won't do. I don't know what I was thinking. I'll go back to town right now and see what else they have."

A second later Antonio was gone, and Q'Bita turned back to Hadleigh.

"Are you okay? Did you get cut?"

Hadleigh was still staring in the direction Antonio had left.

"That… that's him. That's Tony. What was he doing here?"

Jamie and Q'Bita exchanged worried glances.

"Holy shit. This ain't good, Q'B-Doll."

"I know. Stay here with Hadleigh. I'm going to go have a chat with Antonio."

Q'Bita rushed off the porch, grabbed Rene by the arm, and pulled him in the direction Antonio had left. They rounded the corner just as Antonio's car shot out of the parking lot in a shower of crushed gravel and dust.

"Sweet Sisters of Mercy, we could have been stoned like wayward sinners just now. Stay here. I'll grab my keys and we can run him down like The Rock in that bounty hunter movie. Lord have mercy, I love his guns," Rene said.

"No, Rene. Let's go talk to Hadleigh first. If Antonio is Tony, I think I'd better call Andy and let him handle this."

Over the next ten minutes Hadleigh recounted everything she knew about Tony and assured them she was certain he and Antonio were the same person.

Rene and Jamie took her inside to get something a little stronger then iced tea to calm her nerves while Q'Bita called Andy.

Andy picked up on the second ring.

"Hey, Q'Bita, I was just thinking about you. How's everyone doing over there?"

"Well, not so great. I need to tell you something, but you have to promise me you won't get upset."

There was a pause and Andy said, "Okay, go on."

"I know you've been trying to get hold of Hadleigh, and I should have told you she was coming here, but I wanted to see if she'd tell me anything more about Tony."

"And?"

Q'Bita could hear the agitation creeping into Andy's voice and figured it was best to get to the important part quickly.

"Tony is Antonio Vartan."

"What? Liddy Lou fostered him, and gave him a job, when no one else in town was willing to give him a chance. Why would he steal from her?"

"I have no idea, but Hadleigh saw Antonio and freaked out. It was obvious he recognized her as well. He was acting cagey and couldn't get away from us fast enough. Rene and I went looking for him and saw him peeling out of the driveway."

Q'Bita heard a knocking sound and Mike Collins' voice, but she couldn't make out what he was saying.

"Tell her to hold a second and I'll be right with her."

"Q'Bita, I gotta take this call; it's about the background check on Hadleigh. I'll send Mike out to look for Antonio and see if we can bring him in for a chat. I'll give you a call later and fill you in."

Andy hung up and Q'Bita went inside to check on Hadleigh. Jamie was in the kitchen loading the dishwasher.

"Where's Hadleigh?"

"She said to thank you for lunch, and she's sorry for making a scene, but she felt it was best if she left. I asked her to stay but she seemed anxious to get home. How'd it go with Andy?"

"I don't think he was happy with me but he's going to try to track down Antonio and question him."

"I can't believe he'd turn on Liddy Lou like this. Do you think he really killed Macie over all this?"

"I'm not sure what to think. It's possible, I guess. Andy promised to call later, so we'll just have to wait and see what happens."

"Are you going to tell Liddy Lou?"

"No. For now I say we keep this between us. Oh, crap. Where's Rene? I don't want him blabbing this until we know exactly what's going on."

"I think he went back to the cottage. He said this was all just too much for his delicate psyche to handle and he needed to nap."

Q'Bita's cell phone rang. She was surprised to see it was Andy.

"Hey, Andy. That was quick."

"Hello again. By any chance, is Hadleigh still there?"

"No, she left while we were still on the phone. Why? Is something wrong?"

"I can't talk right now but I'll stop by in a while if you're going to be around."

"I'll be here, and I'll make sure there's pie."

"You're a good woman. Talk to you soon."

Q'Bita hung up and noticed Jamie was staring at her.

"What was that about?"

"I'm not sure but I don't think it was good."

Chapter 32

Andy hung up the phone and tried to quell the angry feeling rising inside him. He'd already snapped his pencil in half and cut his knuckle. He took a deep breath and reminded himself to not choke Chance before he got to the bottom of things.

He walked to the door and opened it like a normal, not furious, person. Chance was sitting at his desk, feet propped up on the corner like it was his Pappy's porch rail, talking on his cell phone.

Chance looked up at Andy then went right back to talking on his phone.

"Chance, if it isn't too much trouble, I'd like a word with you. In my office. Now."

Andy was sure his words had come out with enough vitriol Chance got the point he wasn't pleased. Chance had always been a pain in Andy's ass but this time he'd gone too far, and Andy wasn't about to let this one slide.

Chance stopped in the doorway and leaned on the frame looking unfazed.

"What's got your panties all bunched up, big guy?"

"Chance, I'm not really in a joking mood right now. Close the door and sit your ass down."

For once, Chance didn't give him any lip and did what Andy asked.

"I just got off the phone with Helen Kim at the State Records' office. Anything you'd like to share with me before I continue?"

Chance shifted a little in his chair but said nothing.

"Okay, then. Maybe you can tell me why she seems to think I've already requested a full background search on Hadleigh Banks, because I sure as hell don't remember requesting it."

"I'm guessing you already have that figured out or we wouldn't be having this delightful conversation."

"Chance, I'm done playing games with you. I want everything you got from the State, or anywhere else for that matter, and I want to know everything you've shared, or discussed, with Red Dixon about this case. If I even suspect you're holding anything back, I'll charge your ass with obstruction."

Chance got up, went to his desk, then came back and slapped a thick folder down on Andy's desk.

"There you go, boss. It's everything I've got."

Chance turned and started to walk away.

"Where the hell do you think you're going? We're not done here."

"You may not be done, but I am. If you can't look at that file and figure it out for yourself then maybe you should step aside and let someone more competent be sheriff."

"Chance I've seriously reached the end of my patience with you. I get you don't care for me, and frankly I don't give a rat's ass. What I do care about is finding out what really happened to Macie Dixon and making sure whoever did it goes to jail. I'm gonna give you two choices, and you'd better choose wisely. You can either sit down and explain this mess to me or you can leave your gun and badge on your way out. It's up to you."

Chance took off his badge, unholstered his gun, and laid them both on Andy's desk. Andy picked up Chance's badge.

"You'd better be sure about this, because you won't be getting this back."

"I won't need it. The election is only a few months away, and I'll be wearing your badge after that. I'd tell you to keep it, you might need it for yourself, but I think we both know that won't work out. Maybe your girlfriend can find a job for you at the Red Herring Inn."

It took every ounce of self-control Andy had not to come across the desk and punch Chance in the face.

Chance's cell phone rang in his pocket. He looked at the screen and then looked directly at Andy as he answered.

"Hey, Red. Great timing. Sure, I can stop by. My schedule just became wide open."

Chance waved over his shoulder as he left Andy's office, and Andy had a split-second urge to shoot him in the back with his own gun.

Andy kicked his trash can across the room. It ricocheted off the wall and rolled out into the bull pen. He let loose a string of profanities and suddenly felt much better.

His Aunt Maggie appeared in the doorway and glanced at the gun and badge lying on his desk.

"What's that all about?"

"I just removed a 180-pound hemorrhoid from my back side. Doesn't hurt as much as you'd think it would."

Maggie laughed then asked, "You're okay?"

"Yeah, I'm all good."

"Great, then get back to work. I need you to find out who killed Macie Dixon before I get stuck being Evie Newsome's new bridge partner. She plays for blood, and I'm just there for the snacks."

Andy locked Chance's gun and badge in his safe and put the file Chance had given him in the box with everything else they had on the case so far. If Red was going to break the rules, then he sure as hell couldn't say anything if Andy bent a few of them, too. It was about time both sides had all the evidence.

He'd called Q'Bita on the way and let her know he was coming. She'd promised to make sure they had enough pie to hold them over while they combed through the evidence.

When Andy arrived at the Red Herring Inn, Q'Bita greeted him with a hug and two kinds of pie. Some of his earlier tension started to drain away and he wondered for a minute if this was what it would be like to come home to Q'Bita every day. He liked the way this felt.

Q'Bita was sitting across the counter from him watching him eat a second slice of pie. She reached her hand across the counter and rubbed his forearm.

"When you've finished with this slice, maybe it would be better if we went up to my suite. I think we'll have more privacy than we would here."

As if on cue, Tom and Kari entered the kitchen. When Kari spotted Andy, she stopped so quickly Tom ran into the back of her.

"Hello, Andy. What a nice surprise. I hope this is a social call and not police business."

"Mom, please," Q'Bita said.

"I'm not trying to be impolite, Q'Bita. It's just hard to tell lately whether he's here as Andy or as Sheriff Hansen."

Kari's expression was a mixture of hurt and anger, and Andy couldn't tell if she was going to slap him or start crying. Fortunately, Tom knew exactly how to defuse the situation.

"I think what your mother means to say is that both versions of Andy end up cleaning us out of pie so it's hard to tell them apart."

Tears started to stream down Kari's face as she took a step closer to Andy.

"I'm sorry. Tom's right, I didn't mean to be rude."

"It's alright. You don't need to apologize, Kari. I know how hard this has been on all of you and I don't blame you for wanting to wring my neck. If it's any consolation, I swear to you, I am not going to rest until I clear Liddy Lou. I know she agreed to the plea deal because she thinks she's protecting you guys, but I'm more convinced than ever she's being set up, and I'm not going to let her take the fall for something she didn't do."

Kari sniffled and nodded her head but was too choked up to speak.

Andy glanced at Q'Bita and was relieved to see she'd relaxed a little.

"We're gonna grab some wine and snacks and head over to Beecher and Rene's to watch a movie if you'd care to join us," said Tom.

"Thanks, Daddy, but I think Andy and I are gonna pass for tonight. Maybe next time."

When they were finally alone in Q'Bita's suite, Andy told her about his falling out with Chance and how Chance had been feeding information about the case to Red.

"But I still don't understand why Chance ordered the background search on Hadleigh when he and Red both seem convinced my nana killed Macie."

"That's the interesting part. It wasn't just a criminal background check. He ran a DNA profile, too. I'm guessing we'll find the answers somewhere in the file he gave me."

"So this is all evidence from the case?"

"Yep. I'm not supposed to share this outside the department, but Chance has already shared it with Red and his lawyers, which gives them an unfair advantage and proves I can't trust my own people. It also means I don't feel the least bit bad about letting you see what we have so far."

The first part of the file contained background and criminal records information and didn't reveal anything different from what Jamie had already uncovered. Andy laid the DNA results out on the coffee table so they could look at them together.

"You're the one with the fancy science degree so you'll probably understand these more than I will," Andy said.

"My Masters is in Food Science. I'm afraid that's not all that useful for solving murders."

As they read through the report it became clear the DNA was used to test familial relationship. As they reached the end, they were both shocked to see the summary section of the report.

"Oh, you have to be shitting me," Andy said.

"Oh my God, Andy, does this say what I think it does?"

"Well, if you think it says that there is a 99 percent certainty that Red Dixon is Hadleigh Banks' father, then yes."

"Do you think Hadleigh knows this?"

"I'm sure she does. This is based on blood samples that were submitted recently, and she would have needed to consent to the testing."

"I knew she was holding back something. I assumed it was about Tony; that's why I invited her over again. Then she saw Antonio and it was obvious they recognized each other so I just assumed that was it. I guess I was way off base. Speaking of Antonio, any luck tracking him down?"

"Nope. It's like he disappeared off the grid. He didn't return to his place, and his cell phone is turned off. We'll find him sooner or later."

They sat in silence for a few minutes as they both reread the DNA results.

"So does this have any impact on my nana's case?"

"It could. Learning she's Red Dixon's daughter gives Hadleigh a few millions dollars' worth of motive to kill Macie."

"So, what now?"

"Now we go back through this box and see if we can tie Antonio or Hadleigh to any other evidence."

They spent the next hour looking through stacks of paper and interview transcripts and found nothing that implicated Antonio, and only the smallest mention in Patti Becker's statement about Hadleigh and Macie's argument.

Andy got up to use the bathroom, and Q'Bita poured them each another glass of wine. She pulled the box closer to see if there was anything else inside and found a folder labeled crime scene photos.

"What are you looking at?" Andy asked.

"The crime scene photos. They were still in the box."

"Sorry. Some of them are pretty graphic, and I didn't want to put you through that."

"I'm tougher than I look. I'll be fine."

Andy laid them out on the table. Most weren't that shocking but the few showing Macie's body lying face down in the hallway were hard to look at. Q'Bita looked them over several times then picked up two of the pictures and looked at them closer.

"So the cause of death was strychnine poisoning, and these cinnamon buns are supposedly how Macie ingested the poison?" Q'Bita asked.

"Yes, that's the current working theory."

"Are the tox results somewhere in this pile?"

Andy shuffled through the pile of paper and handed her the tox results.

"What are you looking for?"

"Something about the color of the cinnamon in these pictures is bothering me, and I'm hoping the tox results will back up my suspicion."

Q'Bita glanced down the page and finally spotted what she was looking for.

"I knew it. Andy, there's no way my nana made these cinnamon buns, and the tox results prove it. My nana is deathly allergic to cassia cinnamon. The coumarin levels in these tox results are huge, which tells me whoever made these cinnamon buns used a ton of cassia cinnamon. That's the common, inexpensive kind you find in grocery stores. The reason our guests love our cinnamon buns so much is because we use a special blend of spices I created for Nana. It only contains trace amounts of Ceylon cinnamon, which has extremely low levels of coumarin. Our spice blend also contains nutmeg, ginger, cardamom, and white pepper, none of which showed up on the tox results."

"Okay, but couldn't Liddy Lou have just worn gloves when she made them, so she didn't come in contact with the cinnamon?"

"No. You don't understand. When I said she was deathly allergic I meant that literally. She breaks out in hives and goes into anaphylaxis if she touches cinnamon or breathes it in. She keeps an EpiPen in her purse just in case she comes in contact with it while she's out and about. It takes hours for her to recover if she gets sick."

Andy looked like a light bulb had finally gone off in his head.

"Which means she couldn't have made the cinnamon buns,

dropped them off at the studio, then given herself an injection, and showed back up on the security camera footage looking just fine all in the span of a few hours."

"Exactly," Q'Bita said with a smile.

"Wow, not bad. If you ever decide to give up Culinary Forensics and the Red Herring Inn, let me know. I have an opening for a deputy and you'd make a great fit. Probably look good in the uniform, too."

"I think it's best if I stick to making pie and let you carry the gun."

"Speaking of pie, all this talk of cinnamon is making me hungry, and I haven't had a slice in at least two hours."

Q'Bita grabbed Andy a slice of the pie she'd brought up from the kitchen and put on a pot of coffee hoping the caffeine would keep them going for a while.

While Andy devoured his pie, Q'Bita looked through the evidence again for anything they might have missed.

"See anything else?" Andy asked.

"Nothing we haven't already discussed. So, what's your plan from here?"

"Well, first thing tomorrow I'm going to talk to Orvis and fill him in on your cinnamon theory. He can make some inquiries and get it added to the official record without anyone on Red's team knowing you were involved. Then I'm going to track down Hadleigh Banks and find out why she didn't tell me Red Dixon was her father and see if she's hiding anything else."

Q'Bita sank back into the couch and stifled a yawn. Andy looked at his watch and frowned.

"Wow, it's 1:30. I should probably get going so you can get some sleep."

"Or you could just stay here tonight."

The words flew out of her mouth before she even realized what she was saying, and the look of surprise on Andy's face made her blush.

"Now there's an idea I like even more than I like pie."

Chapter 33

Morning came too quickly and Q'Bita hated the thought of leaving her warm bed and Andy's embrace, but she had a business to run, and he had a murder to solve.

She slipped out of bed and made her way to the bathroom. Before returning to the bedroom, she pulled on her robe and ran a comb through her hair. Andy's presence this early in the morning was going to be entertaining enough for her family. Showing up looking like she'd just been ravished would only make it worse.

She could hear the chatter of her family coming from the kitchen as they crossed the dining room.

"Are you sure you're ready for this?" she asked Andy.

"Are you sure there will be coffee and biscuits?"

As soon as her family saw Andy, the chattering stopped and they all just stared.

Andy leaned forward and placed his hands on her shoulders.

"Don't look now but I think we broke them."

This seemed to snap them all out of their trance.

"Good morning, Sheriff. This is an unusual treat. What brings you by this early in the morning?" Liddy Lou asked with a wicked smile.

Andy didn't get a chance to answer before Rene chimed in.

"If I had to guess I'd say he never went home last night, but that would be just scandalous. Let's hope Spenser Penn doesn't get wind of this."

"Okay, okay. You've all had your fun. Now let's be adults and enjoy our coffee," Q'Bita said.

"Oh, right, coffee. I guess he's not here just for your buns."

"That will be enough sass out of you, Rene. Let the poor man finish his coffee in peace," Liddy Lou scolded.

Andy drained his cup and said his goodbyes to her family then leaned over and kissed Q'Bita on the top of the head. She walked him to his truck, and they shared a long kiss.

"I liked waking up next to you," Andy whispered. "I could get used to it if you want to do it more often."

"Even if it means being harassed by my family while you drink your morning coffee?"

"I could get used to that, too. Well, most of it. The sight of Rene in a purple silk kimono and furry slipper pumps at 7 AM might take a while to get used to."

Q'Bita hugged him again and hated to let go but they'd uncovered a lot last night and Andy needed to get to work on it.

"I'm going to call Orvis on the way in and get him started on the cinnamon, then I'm gonna see about getting Hadleigh Banks back in for questioning. Since I'm down a deputy now, it could be a long day, especially if we locate Antonio and bring him in. I'll try to call you during the day and give you an update if I can."

The rest of the day crawled by as Q'Bita waited for her phone to ring. She'd filled Jamie in when he got there and made him promise he wouldn't tell anyone else in the family until Andy gave them the okay. She didn't want to get her nana or her family's hopes up unless there was something solid to tell.

It was almost 4 o'clock when Andy finally called.

"Hello, gorgeous. How are you hanging in?" Andy asked.

"Well, that depends on what news you have for me."

"I'm afraid I don't have much to tell. Orvis is having the lab run a few more tests but they'll take a day or two. I'm not too worried, though. Orvis pretty much agreed with everything you told me. What does have me concerned is that both Hadleigh and Antonio seem to have disappeared."

"Disappeared?"

"Yeah. I went by Antonio's place this morning on the way in to

155

the station, and his roommate says he hasn't been there since he left for work yesterday. I issued an APB and we've contacted all the bus and train stations nearby, but so far, he hasn't turned up.

"I also had Mike go by Hadleigh's, and he said it looked like she'd left in a hurry. Her closet was cleaned out and there were a few empty picture frames and signs that other personal belongings had been taken. He stopped by the Dixons' place and the maid said she hadn't been around since Macie died."

"Do you think they left town together?"

"For Liddy Lou's sake, I hope neither of them left town, but if they did, I hope both left willingly."

The rest of the afternoon didn't move any faster, and Q'Bita was relieved when Andy finally pulled into the driveway around eight. She went outside to meet him and noticed he looked exhausted.

"Hey, sweetheart," Andy said as he bent to give her a kiss. "It's a nice night. I've been holed up all day. You up for a walk and some fresh air?"

They held hands as they walked. Q'Bita could feel the tension in Andy's grip.

"So, are you going to tell me what has you all worked up or are we just going to keep walking until you explode?"

"I got a call around five from the night manager at the bus station. Seems he sold a ticket last night to a very nervous girl matching Hadleigh's description. He says he remembers her because her purse was open, and he could see a huge wad of cash and a small handgun inside. She asked for a ticket on the next bus leaving Castle Creek and didn't seem to care where it was headed."

"Was she alone or was Antonio with her?"

"She was alone."

"A hand gun and no Antonio. That doesn't sound good at all."

"I'm sorry, Q'Bita. I know you like Hadleigh, but this looks really bad."

"I do like Hadleigh, but I love my nana. If Hadleigh is the killer, then she needs to face the consequences of what she's done."

When they reached the pond at the far end of the property they stayed for a while, watching the stars and listening to the crickets and bull frogs. The sound of Andy's stomach growling finally got them moving again.

They were almost finished with dinner when Andy's phone rang.

"Damn it, it's Mike. I hope to hell he doesn't need me to come back in. I haven't even had pie yet."

Q'Bita could only hear one side of the conversation but the look on Andy's face said he was about to miss that pie.

"I'm sorry, sweetheart, I gotta go. A couple of hikers just came across a car in Cope's Ravine, and there's a body inside. Mike says it sounds like it might be Antonio Vartan."

"Oh my God. No wonder it seemed like he'd disappeared."

"I'll call you as soon as I can, but don't wait up; this could take hours."

Q'Bita tossed and turned most of the night and kept checking her phone but Andy still hadn't called. At one point near morning she must have fallen asleep, because she was dreaming of a giant bumble bee chasing her around the garden. The bee was so close she could feel the vibration of its buzz against her cheek, then it stopped and was replaced with a loud ding that woke her up.

She felt ridiculous when she realized her phone had slipped under her pillow and it had been ringing. She dialed Andy back without listening to his voicemail.

"Hey, Q'Bita, sorry to call so early. Did I wake you?"

"No, I'm up. What happened? Was it Antonio?"

"Yes, but this was no accident. What I'm about to tell you must stay between us. I'd prefer it if you didn't even tell Jamie, at least for now."

"Okay."

"The tire impressions at the scene show Antonio stopped before going over the edge of the ravine, and there were two sets of foot prints near the tire impressions. When we pulled up the vehicle and Orvis got Antonio out there was a lot of blood, too much for this kind of an accident. Orvis did a preliminary examination and found a gunshot wound in the center of Antonio's chest. He estimates time of death to be late yesterday afternoon."

Q'Bita could feel the blood racing through her whole body and she wanted to throw up.

"Q'Bita, you still there?"

"Yeah, sorry. I was just, ugh, I can't even say it. I don't want it to be Hadleigh."

"I know you don't, sweetheart, but people aren't always what they seem."

"So, what's next?"

"I'm headed to the coroner's office now to meet up with Orvis. He's going to do the autopsy and see what else we can find. I sent Mike back to the station to start coordinating the search for Hadleigh. I'm going to do my best to tie this all together as soon as possible. I'll call you when I get a chance."

Chapter 34

Q'Bita didn't have to worry about keeping the details of Antonio's death a secret for long. By 6 PM it was the top story on every news station in the tristate area, and speculation was running rampant. Word had gotten out to the media that Antonio was wanted for questioning in connection to Macie Dixon's death and that he was the former foster child, and current employee, of the main suspect in the Dixon murder.

Their phones had been ringing non-stop with reporters wanting a quote from Liddy Lou or the family.

Q'Bita glanced around the library and noticed her nana had snuck out at some point. She found her sitting on the porch in her favorite rocking chair, sipping a cup of tea.

"Hi, Nana. Mind if I join you?"

"I'd like that, Q'Bita."

"How are you doing?"

"Well, I've been better, that's for certain. Evie's coming over in a bit, and I'm sure she'll find some way to lift my spirits."

"I'm sorry, Nana. I can't imagine how hard this must be on you."

"It's a trial, to be sure. I didn't think it could get much worse than having Red Dixon force me into a plea deal, but finding out Antonio is mixed up in all this, well, that just twists the knife that Red stuck in my heart. I tried so hard with that boy, and I just don't know where I went wrong or what I did that hurt him so much he could do this terrible thing. Lord knows I didn't care for Macie Dixon, but she didn't deserve to die."

Q'Bita heard the screen door open and glanced up to see Jamie looking panicked.

"Hey, Q'Bita. Can you come in here for a minute?"

"What's wrong?"

"Um, nothing. I just need your help with something, is all."

"It's okay, darling. Evie will be here soon. I'll be fine," said Liddy Lou.

Q'Bita followed Jamie into the front office, and he closed the door behind them.

"Okay, what's going on?"

"I just got a call from Hadleigh. She's been trying to reach you. Says she's going to call back for you in a few minutes. She sounds terrified, Q'Bita."

"Damn. I've gotten so many calls today, I've been rejecting them all."

Q'Bita's phone rang and she showed the screen to Jamie.

"That's her. She's in a bus station in South Carolina."

As soon as Q'Bita said hello, Hadleigh started talking.

"Q'Bita, is it true what they're saying on the news? Is Tony really dead?"

"Yes, it's true."

Hadleigh was quiet for a few seconds, and Q'Bita could hear her sniffling like she'd been crying.

"Do they know what happened yet?"

"If you mean do they know he was murdered, then yes, they know. Hadleigh, the man who sold you the bus ticket has already talked to the Sheriff's department, and they're looking for you. It won't be long until they find you. It would be best if you just went to the nearest police station and turned yourself in."

"Looking for me? Why? It's not a crime to leave for my own protection."

"For your own protection? Are you saying you killed Antonio in self-defense?"

"Q'Bita, what are you talking about? I didn't kill anyone. When I saw Tony with Rene, the way he looked at me scared the hell out of me. I went from your house right to Dixon Manor. I wanted them to tell me everything they knew about Tony and those stolen recipes. I've never believed your nana killed Macie, and I think Tony's somehow involved in all this."

"Okay, slow down, you're losing me. What did the Dixons tell you?"

"Well, nothing at first; they weren't there. But a few hours later Mrs. Dixon came to my apartment. That's when she told me how Tony stole the recipes and gave them to Mr. Dixon thinking he could score points with Macie.

"She said Tony got angry when Macie used the recipes but wouldn't go out with him. He tried to blackmail Mr. Dixon over the recipes but Mr. Dixon told him no. Cookie thinks the police have it all wrong, and that Tony killed Macie to punish Red. She said it was only a matter of time until Tony found out that I'm..."

"That you're also Red's daughter."

"You know about that?"

"Yes, and so does the Sheriff's department, and they'd like to discuss it with you."

"Q'Bita, I know how this all looks, but I swear, I told Macie and she understood. The only thing I wanted was to know who my mother was. It wasn't about money. I don't want anything to do with Red Dixon or his money. It ruins everything it touches."

"The man at the bus station said you had a large amount of cash and a hand gun. He saw them in your purse when he sold you the ticket."

"Yes, but I haven't touched the money and the gun isn't mine. I don't even know how to use a gun. Guns scare me. Mrs. Dixon gave me the money and the gun when she suggested I leave town."

"Cookie suggested you leave?"

"Yes. I wanted to go to the sheriff, but she said if I did he might think I was working with Tony and arrest me. She didn't think it was fair Mr. Dixon should have to lose both his daughters."

Q'Bita wasn't sure how she could tell, but she felt certain Hadleigh wasn't making this up. Yet something still didn't add up.

"Hadleigh, I want you to stay put until I get to the bottom of this. Once I know what's going on, Jamie or I will call you back and let you know it's safe to come home."

Hadleigh agreed, but Q'Bita couldn't tell if she really meant it or not. They ended their call and Q'Bita relayed Hadleigh's story to Jamie.

"So what do we do now?" Jamie asked.

"Now we call Andy and let him know where Hadleigh is, so he can have someone pick her up."

"But I thought you said you believe her."

"A big part of me does, but she's wanted, and walking around with a gun in her purse that might be a murder weapon. Turning her in is the safest thing for her. If I'm wrong, and she did kill Tony, then turning her in is the safest thing for the rest of us."

"Okay, so we turn her in. Then what?"

"I need you to stay here near the phone and keep an eye on things while I go have a heart-to-heart with Cookie Dixon. I don't know if it's the protective step-mother thing or Cookie parting with a wad of cash that has me suspicious, but something just doesn't feel right to me. If she's so concerned about Red losing another daughter I'm curious to know why she'd want Hadleigh to leave town."

Q'Bita tried calling Andy twice on the way to Dixon Manor but both calls went to voicemail. She left him a message to call her as soon as possible, then hung up and called the station.

She spoke to Maggie, who said Andy was back out at the crime scene doing a final walk-through, and transferred her to Mike, who promised to contact the local police in South Carolina and have them pick up Hadleigh.

Chapter 35

Andy finished the final walk-through with the crime-lab folks and released the scene. He reached down to pull his phone out of its leather side holder and realized the holder was empty. He walked to his truck and saw his phone laying on the dash board. The message light was blinking. He'd missed two calls from Q'Bita and one from Clarity Fessler from the lab. He dialed the lab first.

"What have you got for me, Clarity?"

"When Orvis asked me to rerun tox on the cinnamon buns I remembered seeing a folder of recipes in the evidence. I decided to look through them and see if there was a cinnamon bun recipe in there that might tell me what other ingredients to test for."

"Wow, I'm impressed. That's good thinking."

"There's more. We originally dusted the folder for prints but not the recipes themselves. I dusted all the individual recipes and found the prints we'd expect, given who handled the recipes, but on the cinnamon bun recipe there was another set of prints that weren't on the folder or any of the other recipes."

"Interesting. Did you get a match?"

"Yes. They belong to Cookie Dixon."

"Okay. I didn't see that coming. Sounds like I'll be having a chat with Mrs. Dixon in the near future. You're a superstar, Clarity. Don't know what we'd do without you."

Andy was so preoccupied thinking about what Clarity had found, he completely forgot to listen to Q'Bita's voicemail. He was on the way back when he finally swiped the screen to play the voicemail and put it on speaker.

"Hey, Andy. It's Q'Bita. I got a call from Hadleigh and I think we're wrong about her being the killer. She left town because

Cookie spooked her. The gun and cash belong to Cookie. I know you're going to be mad, but I'm headed to Dixon Manor now to talk to Cookie and convince her to come in and tell you what's really going on. Call me as soon as you can."

Andy slapped the steering wheel so hard his fingers stung.

"This woman is going to be the death of me."

He tried calling back, but Q'Bita's phone went straight to voicemail. He tried three more times and still didn't get through. Andy could feel himself starting to panic. He whipped a U-turn in the road and started back towards Dixon Manor.

Chapter 36

As she pulled into the front drive of Dixon Manor, Q'Bita was relieved to see Cookie's atrocious purple sports car—the gaudy Maserati, as Beecher liked to call it. She parked behind it and started for the steps. As she reached the top step, she looked up and saw Cookie glaring at her from the other side of the screen door.

"I don't know what brings you here, Q'Bita, but whatever it is you're wasting your time and you're not welcome. Just turn around and go back to The Pickled Herring or whatever you call that ridiculous motel of yours."

Q'Bita stopped half-way across the porch and planted herself with both hands on her hips. She had too much to lose to let Cookie Dixon intimidate her into leaving.

"It's the Red Herring, and it's an Inn, not a motel."

"Whatever. I knew it was named after some kind of fish."

"The name has nothing to do with fish. Oh, never mind, I'm not here to argue with you."

"Then why are you here?" Cookie asked, sounding annoyed.

"I want to talk to you about Hadleigh Banks and why you told her Antonio Vartan killed Macie but didn't bother to share that information with the sheriff."

Cookie flung the screen door open and stepped onto the porch. She sauntered towards Q'Bita, her stiletto heels making tiny clicking noises with each step. The look on her face gave Q'Bita goosebumps even though it was well over eighty degrees out. Cookie was smiling but there was a mixture of rage and disdain behind her smile that would have looked more at home on a maniacal clown.

"Did it occur to you Hadleigh might be lying? She's not as

innocent and meek as she'd have everyone believe. After Macie caught her stealing and fired her, she tried to convince Red she was his daughter so she could con him out of money. It wouldn't surprise me if she turned out to be the killer. It's quite a coincidence Hadleigh leaves town the same afternoon Antonio ends up shot to death, don't you think?"

Cookie was now standing toe to toe with Q'Bita. Her hand darted out and grabbed Q'Bita's left shoulder like an eagle snatching a fish from a river. Pain shot through Q'Bita's arm as Cookie tugged her towards the door.

"What's a matter, Q'Bita, cat got your tongue? Why don't you come in for a drink? It's the staff's day off, and Red won't be home for another couple of hours, so we'll have the whole house to ourselves."

Alarm bells were going off in Q'Bita's mind and she tried to pull free, but Cookie dug her nails in deeper until the pain made Q'Bita's arm go numb.

"Relax, Q'Bita. I thought you wanted to talk. There's no reason to be so tense."

Cookie shoved Q'Bita through the door so hard she banged into a small hall table containing an enormous flower arrangement in a crystal vase.

Once they were in the foyer Cookie loosened her grip, and Q'Bita wiggled free. She heard splashing water and the sound of something hitting the floor. She spun around just in time to see Cookie swinging the now empty crystal vase towards her.

She tried to raise her arm to block the blow but wasn't fast enough. The vase collided with the side of her head and everything went black. Her legs felt like noodles, and she collapsed to the floor. The last thing she remembered was the sound of a slamming door and a dead bolt being engaged.

When she came back around, Q'Bita didn't know how much time had passed. She was tied to a chair in the middle of a large room. Her feet and hands were bound, and she'd been gagged. Her head swam as she tried to look around for Cookie, and she fought the urge to retch.

"Oh, good, look who's finally awake."

Cookie's voice was coming from somewhere behind her. Q'Bita heard a chair scrapping across the floor, and Cookie suddenly appeared in front of her. She placed the chair across from Q'Bita and sat down. In one hand she held Q'Bita's cell phone, and in the other a huge butcher knife.

"Ouch. That's a pretty nasty bump you got there. How're you feeling, Q'Bita? What's that? Oh, silly me, you can't talk with all that fabric stuffed in your mouth. Not to worry, I'll talk, and you can just listen.

"While you were napping I took the liberty of looking at your call logs and noticed you were smart enough to call Andy before coming here. He called back a few times and even texted to say he was on his way here. I hope you don't mind but I didn't want him to interrupt our girl time, so I texted him back and told him no one was home when you got here so you went back to the Inn. I even told him your battery was almost dead and asked him to meet you at home. See, I think of everything. Well, almost everything. I didn't count on anyone connecting enough dots to tie me to this mess, but here you are, and now I'm going to have to improvise."

Q'Bita struggled against her bindings and managed to move her chair an inch or two away from Cookie.

"Wiggle all you want, Q'Bita, but in case you didn't notice, I'm the one with the big knife."

Cookie reached out and took a nick out of Q'Bita's forearm with the tip of the knife, drawing blood.

"Sorry, I just thought it might be a good idea to let you know the sight of blood doesn't bother me. Especially someone else's. Now, if you promise to be a good girl, I'll remove the gag. Don't bother screaming; no one will hear you. This room used to be a wine cellar. Except for those little half windows on the far wall, it's below ground and well insulated."

Cookie raised the knife towards Q'Bita's face, and Q'Bita tried to pull away.

"Hold still. I'm not going to hurt you, at least not yet."

With a quick flick of her wrist Cookie sliced the fabric, and it fell away from Q'Bita's face.

"You can't possibly think you're going to get away with this. People know where I am."

Cookie threw her head back and laughed.

"I hate to break it to you, Q'Bita, but this isn't one of your parents' pathetic books. You may think of yourself as the heroine but there's no happy ending here for anyone but me. And for the record, you'd be surprised at what I've been able to get away with over the years."

"You killed Antonio, didn't you?"

"Very good. What gave me away?"

"Earlier, on the porch, you knew Antonio had been shot to death. The manner of death hasn't been made public yet."

"Dang, you are good. Since we're having such a nice chat, I'm curious what else you've figured out."

"Well, you obviously weren't trying to protect Hadleigh or you wouldn't have given her the gun you used to kill Antonio, so I'm guessing you were trying to frame her for his murder."

"It's too bad I'm going to have to get rid of you. You'd make a much better sheriff than Andy Hansen or Chance Holleran. Red's wasting his money backing Chance."

"But Hadleigh is Red's daughter. Why would you want to frame her?"

"Okay. Apparently, you're not that good or you'd realize the answer to your question is in the question itself."

Q'Bita's head hurt, and she was more concerned with how to get loose than playing riddles with Cookie.

"Oh, for God's sake, Q'Bita, do I have to spell it out for you? Hadleigh wasn't just another scam artist. She actually is Red's daughter, which means she's a legitimate heir."

Q'Bita's phone dinged in Cookie's hand, and Cookie looked down at the screen. Her lips moved, and an angry look spread across her face as she read the text. She stood up, looming over Q'Bita.

"Well, now, this is unfortunate. Seems I wasn't as convincing as I thought. Andy's realized you're not at the Inn and is worried you're headed back here. He wants you to pull over and wait for him because my fingerprints turned up on a cinnamon bun recipe and he thinks I might be involved in both murders. Gosh, Q'Bita, you two are like a crime-fighting duo. When do you have time for sex?"

As the weight of Cookie's words pressed themselves into Q'Bita's brain, a sudden and sickening realization began to form in her gut.

"Oh, God, you killed Macie, too?"

"Yes, I killed Macie. That insipid brat ruined my life from the minute she was conceived. Carlie Haskins was a whore and used the oldest trick in the book to snag Red's money. Not that I didn't do the same thing, mind you, but Red's mother wasn't about to have her son marry a piece of trash like me. I had to leave town and fend for myself while Carlie married Red and pretended they were the perfect little family.

"Unfortunately, for Carlie, I got tired of waiting for their marriage to implode and took matters into my own hands. Now I'm Mrs. Red Dixon, and Carlie and Macie are no longer between me and Red's money."

"You did this for money?"

"Don't look so shocked. People have killed for less."

Q'Bita knew she had to keep Cookie talking until she figured out how to get free or Andy got there. If Cookie was telling the truth, she'd just confessed to killing Macie and possibly having something to do with Macie's mother's death, as well. The only reason Cookie would feel secure enough to spill her secrets would be because she wasn't planning on Q'Bita living long enough to tell anyone.

"Are you saying Macie's mother didn't commit suicide?"

"Give the girl a prize. Carlie Haskins may have had good breeding, but she was hardly a mental match for me. Once I found out she had postpartum depression, helping her end her suffering was almost too easy.

"Of course, that left poor Red on his own to raise Macie, and he was only too happy to welcome me back into his life. I tried to like Macie at first, but she was as needy as her mother. Red spoiled her rotten and threw money at one thing after another, anything to make princess Macie happy.

"I knew she'd depend on Red to pay her way for the rest of her life. You can't imagine how much money we've sunk into this idiotic Macie Dixon Line crap. I wasn't about to let her throw the whole thing away by giving those recipes back to Liddy Lou."

Cookie paced back and forth while she talked, then stopped directly in front of Q'Bita.

Cookie's facial expression had grown sour again. Q'Bita knew she was running out of time and needed to make her move soon. Cookie cocked her head and looked at Q'Bita like she was just realizing something for the first time.

"Ya know, everything would have worked out just fine if you hadn't started snooping around Hadleigh. Why couldn't you just leave well enough alone, Q'Bita?"

Cookie drew the knife up and over her shoulder. Q'Bita could see the wild look in her eyes as Cookie lunged forward, closing the gap between them.

The knife swung down, and Q'Bita made her move. Pushing as hard as she could with her feet, she felt the chair start to tip backwards.

She shifted her weight, threw her shoulders against the back of the chair, and was relieved to feel the chair fall backwards.

Cookie howled in pain as the front legs of the chair collided with her shins and she stumbled backwards. The heel of one of her stilettos snapped and she lost her balance.

A few seconds later they both crashed to the floor. They lay still for a moment then Cookie started to stir.

"You're going to pay for that, you little bitch."

While Cookie was trying to get her feet under her, Q'Bita spotted the knife a few inches away. Cookie hadn't seen it yet. Q'Bita rolled on to her side, which sent a ripple of pain through her left shoulder that almost made her faint.

She glanced over her shoulder and saw Cookie was almost on her feet. Q'Bita tried to wiggle her way towards the knife but the chair wasn't making it easy. From a few feet away, Cookie made a noise like a wounded coyote. Q'Bita could hear Cookie snarling as she moved towards her.

"Now, let's try this again shall we?"

Cookie leaned forward and picked up the knife, then stooped down beside the chair.

"Since you're the chef, why don't you tell me where I should start cutting such a big piece of meat?"

Q'Bita's whole body tensed as she felt the tip of the knife pierce the skin just below her shoulder and she tried to steel herself for what was coming next. But what came next wasn't pain, it was the sound of car doors closing. It was a small sound, but Cookie had heard it, too. She swore, pulled back the knife, and stood up. Q'Bita heard another noise. It sounded like footsteps somewhere above them, coming closer.

Q'Bita screamed as loud as she could, hoping Cookie was wrong about the room being completely soundproof.

"Shut up, you stupid cow. I haven't managed to kill you yet, and I don't need someone else coming down here that I'll have to kill. I'm running out of people to blame this shit on."

The footsteps were practically on top of them now, and Q'Bita screamed again.

Cookie yanked the chair upright then grabbed Q'Bita by her hair.

"If you don't quit making noise I'm going to cut your tongue out and feed it to you."

171

A door opened and Q'Bita heard voices.

"No, Mr. Dixon, you need to let me go first."

"Cookie? Cookie, are you down there?"

Q'Bita recognized the first voice as Mike Collins and the other as Red Dixon.

"Damn it, now look what you've done," Cookie said as she pressed the knife against Q'Bita's throat.

A second later Red and Mike reached the bottom of the steps on the far side of the room.

"Cookie, what are you doing?" Red cried.

"Get back, both of you, or I'll open her throat."

"Mrs. Dixon, I don't want to hurt you so please let go of Miss Block and put the knife down."

Cookie made a snorting sound and Q'Bita could feel the blade of the knife take a small bite of her skin and a trickle of blood run down her neck.

"What are you going to do, Mike, shoot me? We both know you don't have the balls."

"With all due respect, Mrs. Dixon, you are incorrect. I'm going to count to three, and if you don't lay the knife down I'm going to shoot."

Mike started to count, and Cookie tightened the grip on Q'Bita's hair. Q'Bita was holding her breath as Mike spoke.

"One, two… Come on, now, Mrs. Dixon. I'm serious."

Just as Mike was about to say three, Red lunged for him, knocking him to the ground.

Cookie was distracted by their scuffle and loosened her grip on Q'Bita's hair but kept the knife pressed against her neck.

Out of the corner of her eye Q'Bita saw movement from just outside the small windows in the far wall.

She saw a flash of orange, then heard breaking glass.

A second later, Cookie released her grip on Q'Bita's hair and the knife clattered to the floor. Cookie's face was frozen in a look of shock as a pool of red spread across her chest, and she fell to the floor.

Red scrambled to his feet and ran to Cookie. He knelt beside her and scooped her up in his arms.

"Baby, why? Why?" Red cried.

Q'Bita heard Andy's voice from outside the broken window yelling for Mike.

"Mike, help Q'Bita. I'm coming in."

Mike scrambled over to her and started to cut the bindings on her hands and feet. She could hear Andy running across the floor above them, then down the stairs.

Red was still crying, and Cookie was mumbling something to him, but Q'Bita couldn't make out the words.

"Mike, I called EMS on my way here. Go up and meet them. Get them down here the second they pull in. Cookie doesn't look good."

"Damn you, Hansen, you didn't have to shoot her. She would have listened to me," Red sobbed.

Andy helped Q'Bita out of the chair. He wrapped her in his arms and hugged her so tight she could hardly breathe.

"Baby, are you okay?"

"I, I don't know. Everything happened so fast."

Red was still sobbing uncontrollably, and Cookie had stopped making any noise. Andy picked up the chair and sat it near the bottom of the stairs.

"Q'Bita, sit here for a minute. I need to secure the scene and take care of Red, then I'll have Mike take you to the hospital to get those cuts looked at."

The next hour was a blur of EMS and crime scene people moving in and out of the room. EMS did the best they could, but Cookie was gone. At some point someone had placed a blanket over her shoulders, but Q'Bita was still too numb to feel warm or cold.

"Miss Block, how are you doing? The boss man wants me to get you over to the county ER to get checked out. Can you stand okay or do you need help?"

"Thank you, Mike, but I'm fine, really. I just want to go home and get a hot shower and see my family."

Mike turned and looked at Andy, who excused himself and made his way over to them.

"Sweetheart, I know you've been through a lot today, but I need you to go with Mike. This is still an active investigation, and I need you to let the ER folks photograph and document all those injuries. After that you can head home, and I'll be over as soon as I can, okay?"

"Andy, Cookie admitted to killing Macie."

"Yes, I know. When we pulled Antonio's truck up the bank we found a dash cam. The crime scene guys were able to pull audio and video. It captured Antonio asking Cookie for money to keep his mouth shut about her killing Macie. Cookie told him that he was the only one who knew what she'd done, and he wouldn't be telling anyone, then she shot him.

I'll call Judge Tanner as soon as we're done here and ask him to make the arrangements to have your nana's plea deal resolved."

Andy reached in his pocket and handed a set of keys to Mike.

"Here. When you take Q'Bita home you'll need these to remove Liddy Lou's tracker."

Q'Bita had never been so relieved. She slumped back in the chair as exhaustion washed over her, and she had to fight to stifle a yawn. Andy bent over and gave her a deep kiss, then told Mike it was time for them to go.

Chapter 37

It had been a week since Cookie'd tried to kill her, and things were starting to get back to normal. Q'Bita leaned back against the porch railing and took in the sight of all her loved ones gathered around the picnic table destroying a low country crab boil.

As usual, Evie and Rene were badgering each other about something, while Andy and her father discussed strategy for their next poker night. Evie's husband, Putt, was wrestling a crab, and the crab was winning. Beecher and Jamie were guarding the shrimp from Rolfie, who'd already stolen at least a half dozen, but the sight that most made her heart swell with joy was her mother sitting quietly with one arm wrapped around her nana.

The sound of a car approaching drew her attention. She walked down the stairs and greeted Hadleigh with a wave and a smile.

"Thank you again for inviting me, Q'Bita. Are you sure your family is okay with me being here?"

"Hadleigh, nothing that happened was your fault, and without your help I doubt the truth would have come out in time to keep my nana from going to jail."

"That's nice of you to say, Q'Bita, but I still can't help thinking if I wouldn't have come looking for my parents none of this would have happened."

"Oh, Hadleigh, please don't think that way. Cookie wasn't well, and she set this chain of events in motion years ago, when she killed Macie's mother."

Hadleigh looked down at the ground, avoiding eye contact with Q'Bita.

"I guess you're right. I'm not sure what was a bigger shock for Red—finding out Cookie killed his first wife and daughter or that she'd hid my existence from him all these years."

Q'Bita felt uncomfortably stupid and wasn't sure what to say.

"I'm sorry, Hadleigh. Andy told me that just before she passed, Cookie told Red she's your mother. That must have been quite a shock for both of you."

"Yes, it was."

"How is your father doing?"

"Okay, I guess. We haven't talked much since the services for Cookie. I'm meeting with his lawyers next week to finalize the paperwork giving me control of the Macie Dixon Line, but I don't think he's gonna be there."

"Beecher told me you're planning on keeping the business going. He and Rene are so looking forward to working with you."

"I'm looking forward to it, too. I think Macie would be proud to see something positive come from all the hurt that's happened."

"I'm sure she would."

Jamie waved to Hadleigh, and Q'Bita noticed her face light up as she waved back.

"Why don't you go eat? I'll be out soon with dessert."

A familiar voice behind her said, "I hope dessert includes pie."

"Hello, Sheriff Hansen," Hadleigh said.

"Miss Banks. I think you'd better get over there and grab some food before Rolfie eats all the shrimp."

A sense of contentment washed over Q'Bita as she watched her family welcome Hadleigh. She sighed then looped her arm through Andy's.

"They're going to be busy for a while so why don't you follow me inside? I have something in mind I think you'll enjoy more than pie."

Epilogue

He sat at his desk and looked out over the city of Lyon. He was lost in thought when a rapping at the door brought him back to the present.

"Entre."

"Hey, boss, you got a second?"

"Oui, Henri, and I must say your American accent is developing well."

Henri blushed and stepped inside.

"There's been a situation with the Americans you asked me to keep an eye on."

He spun the chair around so fast he almost pitched himself out of it.

"Oui? What's happened?"

Henri laid a folder on the desk in front of him. He flipped it open and found a news article from the Castle Creek Gazette. He began reading.

"It appears they got themselves entangled in a murder investigation. I was surprised some place so small would have such excitement."

He read through the article and paused to reread the section alluding to a romantic relationship between Q'Bita Block and Sheriff Andy Hansen. He felt anger bubbling up inside and slapped the file shut.

"Good work, Henri. Please continue to keep an eye on these people, and in the meantime do me a favor and compile a dossier on the Castle Creek Sheriff. I want to know everything there is to know about this man."

The End

Sinister Cinnamon Buns

While these cinnamon buns do not include the sinister poison that killed Macie Dixon, they are delicious enough they should be called Sinful Cinnamon Buns.

The recipe may look long, but these buns are super simple to make. The sweet dough recipe is what you'd expect for a basic single-rise recipe. It's the filling and the frosting that make these so sinfully delicious.

I'm a big fan of cinnamon, but I'm a full-on fanatic for speculaas spice. This Dutch spice blend usually contains cinnamon, nutmeg, cloves, ginger, cardamom and white pepper. With the addition of a little orange zest, the whole kitchen will smell like Christmas while the buns are baking.

Sinister Cinnamon Buns

Sweet Dough Ingredients
2 ¾ Cups All Purpose Flour, divided
3 Tablespoons White Sugar
1 Teaspoon Kosher Salt
1 Package Instant Yeast (2 ¼ tsp)
½ Cup Water
¼ Cup Whole Milk
4 Tablespoons Unsalted Butter
1 Large Egg

Filling Ingredients
1 Cup Light Brown Sugar
4 Tablespoons Unsalted Butter – softened/room temperature

2 Teaspoons Speculaas Spice (I use King Arthur brand but any brand will do)
1 Teaspoon Honey
½ Teaspoon of Cinnamon
Pinch of Kosher Salt
Zest of 1 Medium Orange

Frosting Ingredients
8 Ounces of Cream Cheese – softened/room temperature
4 Tablespoons Unsalted Butter– softened/room temperature
1 Cup of Powdered Sugar
¼ Cup Orange Juice (preferably from the orange you zested for the Filling)
1 Teaspoon of Honey
¼ Teaspoon of Vanilla (feel free to use a ½ tsp if you like, but I'm not a big vanilla fan)
Pinch of Kosher Salt

Sweet Dough Steps:
Before you get started, pre-heat the oven to 200 degrees.

In a large bowl combine 2 ¼ cups flour, sugar, salt, and yeast and stir to combine.

In a medium sauce pan, over low heat, combine water, milk, and butter until it reaches 110 degrees. It's best to use an instant read thermometer for this step but if you don't have one, this temperature is roughly the point where the liquid becomes hot to the touch.

Add the liquid to the dry ingredients along with the egg and ¼ cup of the reserved flour. Mix until all the dry ingredients are well incorporated. The dough should be springy but not sticky. If it's sticking to the sides of the bowl, or your fingers, add more flour, 1 tablespoon at a time, until the dough no longer sticks.

Form the dough into a loose ball and transfer it to a bowl that has been lightly sprayed with non-stick spray. Set the dough aside to rest 10-15 minutes while you make the filling.

Filling Steps:
In a medium bowl, combine all filling ingredients and mix until thoroughly combined.

Putting It All Together:
Turn the dough out onto a lightly floured surface and roll into a 9 x 15 rectangle. Cover the dough with the filling, being careful to leave about a ½ inch border on all sides. Starting with one long side, tightly roll the dough into a cylinder and pinch the seam closed. Cut the dough into 12-14 equal pieces and place in a lightly sprayed baking dish being careful not to overcrowd the dish so the dough has room to rise. Loosely cover the top of the baking dish with foil. You may want to use 2 dishes with 6-7 buns in each.

Turn off the oven and place the baking dish inside it. Let the buns rise 45 – 60 minutes until almost double in size.

Make frosting while the buns are proofing.

Frosting Steps:
In a large bowl, combine cream cheese, butter, orange juice, vanilla, salt, and honey. Stir or beat on medium speed with a mixer until thoroughly combined. Scrape down sides of bowl and then slowly add the powdered sugar and beat on medium until light and fluffy.

Final Steps:
When the buns have doubled in size, remove from oven and pre-heat oven to 350 degrees. Bake the buns for 25-30 minutes. Keep an eye on them and if they start to brown on top too quickly, cover with foil to prevent burning. When rolls are done, let sit 10 minutes, then frost.

Simple Art of Simple Syrup

I'm fortunate to have the space for a sizable garden, which allows me to grow more herbs than a family of two could use in a life time, let alone a single growing season. I can't stand to see any of my herbs go to waste so I had to come up with ways to use as many as possible. One of my favorite ways to use my surplus is simple syrup.

Simple syrup, as the name implies, is simple to make, and will elevate any dish, or cocktail, from ordinary to unforgettable.

The base recipe consists of a 1-to-1 ratio of sugar to water. From there you can experiment with different sugars and sweeteners, such as brown sugar or honey, and flavor with herbs, tea, etc. Experimenting is where the art comes in. The base recipe supplies the canvas. You create the masterpiece to suit your tastes.

Last summer I had an abundance of French tarragon and found that just a few sprigs made a wonderful simple syrup. I used it in iced tea, sparkling water, and drizzled over grilled peaches.

Like Q'Bita, I'm a huge fan of rosemary. I grow it in the garden most of the year, and indoors when winter is at its worst.

Add this syrup to lemonade, iced tea, and cocktails or use it to baste pineapple, onions, or cherry tomatoes while grilling.

Rosemary Simple Syrup
1 Cup White Sugar
1 Cup Water
1 Tablespoon of honey (optional, but lovely)
2-3 Three-inch sprigs of fresh rosemary, washed but left whole (I used 3)
Rosemary is a potent herb, so it's better to start with less, and

add more until you reach the balance of sweet and herby you enjoy.

Combine sugar and water in a medium, non-stick sauce pan. Bring to a low boil (just a smidge past a simmer) over medium heat. Stir or whisk continuously to avoid scorching the sugar. When bubbles begin to break the surface, add the rosemary sprigs, give a few quick stirs, and remove from the heat. The syrup will thicken slightly as it cools.

Let the syrup cool to room temperature and then pour the syrup through a fine mesh strainer into a glass jar with lid or an airtight container.

Yields approximately 1.5 cups and can be stored in the refrigerator for two weeks.

About J Lee Mitchell

J Lee Mitchell is the author of The Red Herring Inn Mystery series. She does her writing, cooking, and gardening in the heart of South Central Pennsylvania's Amish Country. When she's not doing these things she dreams of training ninjas.

She enjoys traveling, quilting, hoarding cookbooks, and spending time with the World's most patient and loving significant other.

Visit J Lee Mitchell at jleemitchell.com, sign up to her newsletter, and connect with her via Facebook: https://www.facebook.com/RedHerringInn/

Acknowledgements

This book would not have been possible without the guidance, encouragement, and talent of some very wonderful people. I am forever grateful and in debt to you all.

Thank you, RE Vance, for being the best coach and mentor any writer could hope to have. Thank you, Micki K Jordan, for keeping me accountable, for being the voice of reason, and for all your encouragement and willingness to share your knowledge.

Thank you, Ella Medler, for your excellent feedback and editing.

Thank you, Spencer Pierson, for designing a fabulous cover.

Thank you, Kat Brokaw and Erin Shoemaker, for being there from the beginning and being the best BFFs a girl could ask for. Last but not least, thank you to all my friends and family who have been so supportive for all these years.

Made in the USA
Monee, IL
23 July 2021